Henry Kingsley

Number Seventeen

A Novel: Vol. II.

Henry Kingsley

Number Seventeen
A Novel: Vol. II.

ISBN/EAN: 9783337032203

Printed in Europe, USA, Canada, Australia, Japan

Cover: Foto ©Andreas Hilbeck / pixelio.de

More available books at **www.hansebooks.com**

NUMBER SEVENTEEN

A NOVEL

BY

HENRY KINGSLEY

AUTHOR OF 'THE HILLYARS AND THE BURTONS' ETC.

IN TWO VOLUMES

VOL. II.

London

CHATTO AND WINDUS, PICCADILLY

1875

CONTENTS

OF

THE SECOND VOLUME.

CONTENTS

OF

THE SECOND VOLUME.

NUMBER SEVENTEEN.

CHAPTER I.

DRUMMOND AND CARLINA.

THE door had scarcely closed upon her, when the smiling lawyer, Drummond, began walking up and down the room, more like a lunatic than the extremely keen, cold-blooded man he was. The butler came in and asked if he should clear away. Drummond swore at him and ordered him away. The butler went downstairs and swore *to* the footman, not *at* him. The butler swore that there was not a better master in England than Mr. Drummond, and the footman agreed. For Drummond, with all his villanies, was a very kind man. He used to tell a most intimate acquaintance that he could not bear the sight of sin or sorrow. He committed a vast deal of the one, and saw much of the other.

What was he to do now?—that was the question before him. His aim in life had been to marry Mrs. Arnaud. He had risked his liberty for that; he had become a criminal for that; now the chance, as he thought, had come, and he dared not act. If he told her the truth, she would repudiate him: if he withheld the truth, what chance had he? She might, at any moment, say that he had continued to deceive her after her confidence with him; and he would be as far away from her as ever.

He sat back in his chair, and thought. He was a man eternally thinking and never acting. The time had come for him to act, and to act in the most decisive manner, and yet he could not.

A lie, nay more, a felony had been on his mind for nearly twenty years. That fact had made him drink at night, and go to sleep forgetting the matter. But if a man drinks at night he is crapulous in the morning, and so Drummond always woke with a nightmare more ghastly than any which came to him in his dreams.

He wanted to marry Mrs. Arnaud. Why? That is beyond our power to tell. There was nothing very particular about Mrs. Arnaud. We know her well, but she has nothing about her to make a man desire to marry her. She is a fine showy woman with every possible good quality, save that of consistent truthfulness. But the man who desired, or desires, to marry Mrs. Arnaud, was, or is, a thoughtless man.

Consequently, James Drummond was a thoughtless man.

She would have made him a good wife. Certainly, but for how long? She would have cured him of all evil habits, such as that of drinking, but again, for how long? It is impossible to say, because she never married him. We will return to him as he sat after she had left him:—begging pardon for the digression.

When he looked up, Mrs. Arnaud was not in the chair before him. Silently, another woman had come into the room, and was sitting before him.

'Is that you, Carlina?' he said.

'I suppose that I am one of the most unmistakeable people in the world, and this is I,' she replied.

Most unmistakeable, assuredly. A handsome, very splendid woman. She had a shawl over her head, which made her face look more square and resolute than it would have looked had the vast mass of her coarse hair been freely falling about her shoulders, as was usually the case.

'Have you come here to plague me?' said Drummond.

'Yes,' said the woman, Carlina. 'I suppose you do not love me?'

'No.'

'You love that woman, still, I fear?'

'Yes.'

'What are you going to do about the matter? I will never hurt you, you know; but what will you do?'

'Carlina, shall I tell her the truth? Should I win her by——that way?'

'I cannot tell you. What, on earth, is in the woman? I have seen her, and I cannot see anything in her. Well, come

Drummond, I will tell you what I am going to do with you. I am going to tell the truth.'

'You would not do such a thing as that?'

'I don't know,' said Carlina. 'It might be worth my while to do so. I might make terms with Lord Festiniog.'

'That would be sheer treachery,' said Drummond.

'How have I been treated, Drummond? I ask you, how?' said Carlina. 'Man, there are things which you and I dare not talk of, even to one another. One thing, and one thing only, is in common between us, and that is the Ravenna business.'

'No one knows anything more about that than we do,' said Drummond.

'I beg your pardon,' said Carlina. 'The whole matter is known perfectly well at Ravenna. I can assure you of that fact. In Italy, people can know as much or as little as they like. A scandal like that cannot be hidden.'

'But. woman, George is going to Ravenna. Old Festiniog has told me so to-day; I do not know if the boy is going: George goes.

'To dig himself up?' said Carlina.

James Drummond was not beyond a joke yet. He replied:—

'No, to lay a wreath on his own grave. Mary has asked him to do so. Lord Festiniog, as I said, told me so to-day.'

'The farce might get into a tragedy,' said Carlina. 'Come, take my advice, and make a clear breast of it. What can you possibly gain by keeping the secret?'

'Power over Mary!'

'That is to be thought of,' said Carlina. 'I would not pay this price for any man in the world that you are paying for that woman.'

'Women cannot love,' said Drummond.

'Oh, indeed!' said Carlina. 'Well, I go to another point, you have no power over this woman, none on earth. Knowing what we know, Barri always stands between you and any power over her.'

'Remove Barri.'

'He is in Italy, certainly,' said Carlina, 'but, even there, murder is expensive and dangerous. The removal of Barri is nonsense. Why cannot you be quiet over the matter, at least for a time? I am puzzled myself; if you tell the truth she might hate you; and if you lied and she found out the truth afterwards, she would hate you still more. One way or another, I don't think that she will ever marry you.'

'No?'

'Certainly not.'

CHAPTER II.

LORD FESTINIOG MAKES HIS REVELATION.

ALTHOUGH Lady Rhyader and Lord Festiniog, had many polite quarrels, they liked one another as well as relations generally do. In France, as far as we have observed, relations and connections are very scrupulously polite to one another; in our dear little island, relations, particularly if they are religious, find it necessary to do their duty by being rude, and saying things which no one else would dare to say. That is all for the best, no doubt, although the people in Massachusetts and Vermont do not think so. To avoid being led into an essay on the matter, we merely come back to the simple fact that Lord Festiniog and Lady Rhyader quarrelled continually, but liked one another tolerably well.

They discussed matters very much. She was not a bad tempered woman, but she thought it her duty to be always in mild opposition to the ruling power, whether that power was represented by her husband or her father-in-law. Her belief was that Rhyader was the wisest of human beings, but that he never must be allowed to find it out: consequently they nagged at one another continually. The theory which she advanced to her father-in-law and the world was that he was a fool, who would be nothing without her. She had a profound belief in Lord Festiniog, though she would have died sooner than tell him so. She was an excellent little lady, but was totally unequal to a crisis.

One came, and she never put the matter before her husband; for although she would fight him at times on small matters, yet she was, at heart, afraid of him. She took it straight to Lord Festiniog. Possibly it was the best thing she could have done, for he was in possession of more facts than Lord Rhyader.

Lord Festiniog was at breakfast one morning, with his 'Times,' enjoying himself thoroughly, when his valet threw open the door and announced Lady Rhyader.

'My dear soul,' said Lord Festiniog, sitting carefully on his chair, and not moving, 'What the—— what, on earth, is the matter?'

'My boy,' said Lady Rhyader, sinking into a chair.

'What! Barri?'

'Yes.'

'What has he been doing?'

'Get up and take this letter from me.'

'I can't. Why do you come bursting into my dressing room like a lunatic? Bring it to me.'

Lady Rhyader rammed a letter down before him, retired to her chair, and burst into tears.

She thought that he would be impressed with the letter. He did not appear to be so, at all. This, he said, is part of the nonsense which I have heard before.'

'Do you believe in it?' said Lady Rhyader.

'Partially,' said Lord Festiniog. 'Have you told Rhyader about it?'

'No.'

'That is a pity,' said Lord Festiniog.

'Would you mind going away?—because the fact is that I intend to walk through the whole of this business with a high hand, and I have not got my trousers on. The boy Barri shall be safe: no one shall touch him.'

'But, Lord Festiniog, do you believe this? Is it possible that the woman's words can be true?'

'I can't tell you,' said Lord Festiniog. James Drummond has lied to me more than once, and may have lied now. The woman does not seem to have lied. And, all said and done, Anne, what, in the name of confusion, does it matter? What can possibly befall Barri?'

'He is going to Ravenna with George Drummond.'

'Well, I wish he would go anywhere else' said Lord Festiniog, it is a most unhealthy place.'

'Truly, and if he finds out the truth which this woman says is perfectly well known there, what a safe nurse he would be for the boy.'

'Nonsense, nonsense, Anne, you would never suspect him?'

'What did you know of him before you entrusted my son to his care?'

'I don't know very much of him,' said Lord Festiniog.

'Any one is good enough for Barri, I suppose,' she replied, angrily, 'his father is a dear saint according to this woman; is he not? His virtues may be hereditary.'

'I cannot distrust him.'

'Of course not,' she said, scornfully.

'Now go away, he said, let me dress, and I will see all about it. Meanwhile I will telegraph to stop them going near the place. I will do everything which can be done, but you must let me do it in my own way. Now, go and tell Rhyader, you ought to have told him first.'

'She went, and Lord Festiniog dressed hastily, and ordered his carriage. His valet noticed that he was extremely disturbed; he drove to the nearest telegraph office, and was there for a short time; he had sent a message to Rome, requiring George Drummond not to approach Ravenna, for that it was most unhealthy in the autumn; he was however too late here, though he did not know it: then he got into his carriage again and told the coachman to drive to Ravenna.

'To where my lord?'

'To Ravenna—I mean, to No. 17.'

'In which street, my lord.'

'Fool, are there two number seventeens in the world? There is but one, that in

Hartley Street, and I wish that it had been burnt down before I saw it.'

All this temper and haste had entirely disappeared before he got there. Like a perfect gentleman, as he was, he apologised to his coachman, when he got out, for calling him a fool. He knocked at the private door, and was admitted by Rachel.

'Is your mistress at home?' he said.

'Yes, but Mr. Drummond is with her in the back parlour.'

He at once went out and told his coachman to drive into the square and wait for him, and then, putting a sovereign into Rachel's hand, he bade her silently show him upstairs into Mrs. Arnaud's private apartments.

Rachel was one of those extremely honest and crusty people, so much admired for their frankness, who could have risked her soul for a couple of pounds; more dangerous humbugs do not exist; that sainted piece of virtue slipped Lord Festiniog past the parlour door and up the staircase with the speed and dexterity of an experienced Spanish duenna.

When Mrs. Arnaud came up after her interview with Drummond, she started to find Lord Festiniog there, standing before the fire.

'How on earth did you get here?'

'I bribed your servant with a sovereign. Keep that woman, she is simply worth her weight in gold.'

'I have a good mind to send her to the right-about.'

'Don't do that,' said Lord Festiniog. 'Never part with servants who will tell everything they know for money, they are invaluable. I cannot get them. That woman might be useful. Now sit down to the most important conversation you ever had in your life. To begin with, what has Drummond been saying to you?'

'That is a very long story to tell, and I am loth to begin it; still more loth to end it, because the end will lower me in your estimation. I will tell it to you if you like, for you have always been kind to me. The man has always loved me from the first, but I have never cared for him. I never absolutely disliked him, or we should not have been so intimate. He was very good to me abroad, and afterwards I thought him to be a villain, who was paying attention to me when he was married to another. Such, I now find, is not the case. Well, he has been renewing his suit to me.'

'With what success? It seems strange that he should do so after so many refusals.'

'Well, your family affairs are the cause of it. I felt positively certain that he knew, or could find out something, about these extraordinary letters threatening Barri's life. I wished to get at the truth, and I lied to do it. Now, you will never speak to me any more?'

'Don't talk nonsense, Mary. How did you lie?'

'Not at all in words, but I gave him to think that if he could find the matter out for me, I would look more favourably on him. I never meant to do so, but I wanted to get the secret from him.'

'Have you done so?'

'No. I cannot get him to speak; he will not without a decided written promise from me.'

'Which you have not given?'

'How could I, with the memory of Iltyd in my heart?'

'Oh! please never mind Iltyd; he was undoubtedly a saint; when did you ever hear me say to the contrary? He was my son; and I have always stuck by my family, and paid their debts. Gervase might be fifty times the ass he is, but I would stick by him all the same; Iltyd, however, is dead and buried, try to forget him just now, or at least, don't Balmoralise over him.'

'I will not, then. Drummond has said that he will put me in a position I never dreamt of assuming if I would give him the promise of my hand.'

'What more has he told you?'

'Nothing. I have had such a terrible scene with him, Lord Festiniog. He drinks, at times, but just now he is mad.'

'He has not let out the truth to you, then?'

'I can't say, I do not know what the truth is. The matter lies in a nutshell; he wants to marry me; I will not marry him, and he holds some secret.'

'I have found it out, Mary.'

'Thank God, then, I have nothing more to do with it.'

'I fear that you have, Mary,' said Lord Festiniog. 'Can you cast your mind back to the time when you were at Ravenna?'

'Yes. I do not see any difficulty in doing that: I have told you of those times before.'

'Once again, go through the facts.'

'Well! I went to Ravenna with Carlina. I had my child with me. I fell ill there. I recovered; and the child died, while I was delirious.'

'Drummond was with you?'

'Drummond was with me at first; but it was Carlina who told me of my child's death; then, the doctor confirmed her.'

'Now, Mary, listen to me, and keep your head. Your child never died at all.'

'But I saw his poor little grave.'

'But he did not die, for all that.'

'When did he die then?' said Mrs. Arnaud, very quietly but rather—well—dangerously.

'He is not dead at all,' said Lord Festiniog: 'that is Drummond's great secret, and I have discovered it.'

Mrs. Arnaud burst out laughing.

'My lord,' she said, 'you are perfectly wrong. My poor boy is dead enough.'

'I think that I can prove the contrary,' said Lord Festiniog. 'I feel sure of it. I have had an interview with Lady Rhyader, this morning, who knows what, I think, is the truth, and who is in a state of mind about it;—she always is in a state of mind, you know—but, previous to her coming, I had an almost overwhelming amount of authority in my hands. I have deceived her, but I will not deceive you. Your child never died at all.'

'Then if you allow that, and also allow my marriage, my son would succeed after Barri's removal.'

'Certainly. James Drummond knows it, and has traded on the fact. You can see that now?'

'Perfectly, my lord.'

'Do you remember George Drummond?'

'My lodger, why not?'

'Did you like him?'

'Yes, surely. He was very kind to me the first night I came here. He was in that miserable mistake about Heloise, and suffered for it. I took rather a fancy for him.'

'Mary, that young man is your son.'

There was a dead silence, scarce broken by the passing carriages in the street. She sat with her head bent over the fire, without saying a word. Lord Festiniog rose quietly and withdrew, putting a packet of letters in her hand. When he was gone, she read them.

CHAPTER III.

MARY ARNAUD'S GREATEST TRIAL.

They were simply the letters of the woman Carlina, the ex-mistress of Drummond, who had, in a fit of combined jealousy and avarice, put the whole of the facts before Lord Festiniog, and part of them before Lady Rhyader. Nothing did that excellent woman ever write to Gervase. She knew that he would never believe a word of it, true as it was. She was a countrywoman of Catherine de Medici, and knew perfectly well what she was doing.

The facts were most simple: we see, in

this excellently ordered country of ours, stranger things every day. Drummond wished Mrs. Arnaud to be left alone in the world, and to be dependent on him. He had her child removed. Italy is no better than our unimpeachable England, and no worse. He paid freely, and the child was taken from her.

Carlina was his agent, but she nearly went too far. He had offered her a large reward to do the thing for him. Knowing the certainty of her falling ill at Ravenna, at a certain time of the year, Carlina had persuaded her to go there. She succeeded perfectly.

But she was not a woman in the least degree likely to leave herself without witnesses. More people than she, in Ravenna, knew what had been done; in fact, the matter was so notorious, that she had to divide the money which she got from Drummond amongst those who were in the secret. She always, however, gave Drummond the idea that she was the sole repository of the secret.

It was only when the people, little better than banditti, whom she had employed, got too pressing for her pocket, that she came to London. Drummond had supplied her with money liberally, but she was getting middle-aged, and the continual calls on her worried her. She came to England with Drummond's money, and used it for the purpose of seeing if she could make a better bargain with Lord Festiniog. It seemed hopeless until she found that Drummond, with whom she renewed her acquaintance, was actually thinking of finding agents to remove Barri.

Drummond not only loved the mother, but he loved the son. The boy George

Drummond had been adopted by him, and he, having no children, had taken to the boy. No boy in England had a more affectionate father than George Drummond had in his present father, James Drummond.

He had it in his power to make the boy a possible earl, and at the same time he had it in his power to lay an overwhelming load of obligations on Mrs. Arnaud. In the last interview with her he had hinted very strongly on the latter point, and asked her to give him a promise of marriage on his parting with a secret which would make her the proudest and happiest woman in England, or leave her a melancholy and wretched woman, of doubtful position, for the remainder of her days.

She had been playing with him, and she saw on what terribly dangerous ground she had been walking; not one word had she got out of him about the threats to Barri: he only reiterated that he could discover everything about the matter, if she made him the promise. She ended her trial and his by saying coolly, but with extreme terror, with her hand on the door:—

'James Drummond, I have made up my mind at once and for ever. Sooner than marry you I would be found dead some cold morning in the casual ward of the worst workhouse in the City of London.'

'You distinctly encouraged me the other day' he said, hoarsely yet almost inaudibly.

'For that forgive me, James. I have made my ultimate resolution now. If you could make me a duchess, nothing would alter it. I am going, and, so, good bye.'

'Then, I must serve you in spite of yourself: will you shake hands with me before I go?'

Her heart melted to him suddenly; she came back sobbing, and said: 'God bless you, James Drummond, for your kindness in old times. May God save you from all evil.'

'God!' he said, taking her hand, 'why do not you do it yourself?'

She broke from him, and went upstairs to find the whole mystery cleared up by Lord Festiniog. The man who had been her suitor for twenty-five years, to whom she had just been kind in a moment of pity: this man had inflicted on her the most ghastly injury which man could inflict on woman. He had kept his vile secret in his heart, to use against her, all these years; he had seen her bitter sorrow for her pretty child, and had never relented; he had professed love to her a hundred times; but, now, she saw what kind of love he meant, and cursed her beauty when she thought of it.

She had no pity on the man, of any sort or kind, but a most furious hatred; she felt as though she could have held the hand which had just clasped his, in the fire. To torture her for all these years! to let her kneel on an empty grave, and offer up the purest prayers which ever flowed from human heart! She had prayed on the grave at Ravenna, that when she met Iltyd, purified and ennobled in heaven, her dead child might be with him in the form of a cherub, and that the three might pass into heaven together sanctified. All this, which had been the sentiment of her life, was made foolish, idle, almost absurd, by the selfish lust of a scoundrel.

Her throat was parched, and her hands were clenched, when she thought of what this man had done to her. More awful things came into her head. God had heard her fruitless prayers for her dead child, and had made no sign.

It would have been a bad thing for Mr. James Drummond had he come near No. 17 that night. He could never justify himself; his accomplice, Carlina, had noticed that a certain habit had greatly increased upon him lately, and thought that his life was not to be depended on. After his death, she would be completely ruined. She, therefore, like a keen Italian woman, just threw herself into the hands of Lord Festiniog, stated her case completely, of course, sparing herself as much as possible, and offered to go to Ravenna to prove it further, which she could easily do.

There was no doubt about the matter, as Mrs. Arnaud read through the letters which Lord Festiniog had left with her. He seemed satisfied that there was a strong *primâ facie* case, and had the woman in hand. She, at once, knew it to be true. A hundred acts and hints of Drummond's, a hundred circumstances after her recovery came crowding on her, and made the matter certain for her which might still be doubtful for others.

Yes, that wretch had violated all that was most tender in her nature, and what had she got in return? Even that had not been given to her by him, but by the partner of his crime. What had she in place of her beautiful child?—'George Drummond.'

'What,' she said in her first burst of anger, 'was he to her?' Was there any resemblance in him to Iltyd? She had not seen him enough to judge, and yet she began to see resemblances in voice, features, and manners. She went to her desk and took out the portraits of her husband and her lost child, and sat before the fire to compare them to George Drummond.

It grew late and dark, but she sat, still, brooding over the fire, with the two pictures before her. She tried to pray, once or twice, but she could not. God had allowed her to make fruitless prayers over her dead child, and had made no sign that he was living. The religion which had served her so well, through so many troubles, was suddenly swept away. Mrs. Arnaud went to bed that night, a lonely and desperate woman.

CHAPTER IV.

GEORGE DRUMMOND'S TEMPTATION.

FROM London to Antwerp, from Antwerp to Brussels, from Brussels to Namur, from Namur to Luxemburg, went George Drummond and Barri. Never were two such hearty companions in this world. Barri was, or seemed to be, in paradise. On only one subject was George at all disagreeable: he insisted on Barri speaking French every hour of the day before dinner. After dinner Barri might speak English, but before they had gone very far on their journey, Master Barri found French trip so lightly on his tongue that he preferred it, because he was proud of it: his French was by no means bad, and he had some right to be so. Finding at Strasbourg that German was necessary, he began studying that language, but made little progress in it.

Basle :—the boy complained of Basle as being uncivilised: but then, by a divergence they made to Interlachen, he began to think more about Switzerland. Then, they passed the mountains by the St. Bernard, and saw the monks and the dogs; then, they passed on into Italy, until they came to Rome.

George Drummond at first had liked Barri as he might have liked half a hundred other boys, though, as a rule, he objected to the general run of boys, as mistakes. Barri, however, gained on him. The boy was shrewd, and would not only accept and understand a fact, but would generalise on it. Not always wisely, perhaps, but wisely enough to render an argument necessary, in which case his cousin, unknown as yet as his cousin, got the best, from superior knowledge and, possibly, superior intellect.

At last there came confidence between them. They were lying together in the ruins of the Coliseum, when Barri said:

'George, I wish you would confide in me.'

'About what?' said George Drummond.

'About Heloise, of course. I know all the trouble you had about her. Why do men like you care so much about women? I did not care much for her.'

'You cannot understand these things, child,' said George Drummond.

'No, but I could speak to you about

them when you were sorry. May I? For you have been so very kind to me.

'My poor little Barri,' said George Drummond, 'you may talk as long as you please about Heloise. I have entirely got over that attachment. I loved her very much for a time, and I think that she made a fool of me. But she is far less to me than you are.'

'That is odd,' said Barri.

'Not at all,' said George Drummond. 'I have always thought that I should like to form a mind. Ever since I read Plato, I have thought of what the perfect prince or president should be. You are pure and clever, why should you not form yourself, young as you are, for the splendid position which you will ultimately occupy? Boy, if you did so, you might be prime minister of England. Do not speak any more to me about Heloise or any such people. I am carving my way in the world with desires and ambition before me, of which you cannot, as yet, dream. Your grandfather is no one; your father is a fool; you may do something yet. I would to God I was in your place.'

'I thought that you were still in love,' said Barri.

'That's all gone, my boy. I want a career. I have more than your ability: I want your prestige. You will be Lord Festiniog ultimately. It is doubtful whether I shall ever be in Parliament at all.'

'But you will be rich, George.'

'Rich. Yes, unless my father makes some fiasco. Suppose he was to die to-morrow and leave me unprovided for; suppose he was to leave his money—*Maxima debetis*—elsewhere, where should I be? I don't know what to do, Barri. I am utterly sick of the world.'

'Then, come to church,' said Barri.

'I suppose that is the best thing,' said George Drummond. 'We'll go together.'

It was their first day at Rome, and Barri had seen nothing as yet. Holding tight by George Drummond, he passed through vast crowds, keeping on his feet as well as he could. It was an angry crowd, and they gesticulated at one another, but let them pass. The crowd grew thinner, and Barri found himself beside George Drummond in a vast building, with circular arches and domes which seemed to whirl above his head. There was a height before them of marble steps, down which streamed a crowd of singularly dressed people, some in brown, some in white, some in violet; near to the summit of the eminence which he saw, were groups of men in scarlet; before and below them went up a cloud of incense. Suddenly, an old gentleman in white came forward, and bowing, raised his hands. Barri was puzzled; it was the most awful and splendid thing which he had ever seen.

'Where are we, George?' he asked.

'In St. Peter's.'

'Who is the old man?'

'The Pope.'

So, from town to town, they went on idly. Lord Festiniog's telegram had missed them, and they were free to go where they would. They went to Naples, and it was there that George bethought himself of his promise to go to Ravenna and do what Mrs. Arnaud had asked of him.

Ravenna is a most abominable hole;—one of the most fever-stricken places in Italy—but he did not know that. He and

Barri arrived there to find the Florence telegram sent on, forbidding him to go there. He telegraphed back to say that they had come there. Eight hours after, he received a telegram from Lord Festiniog, ordering him to send Barri back to Rome, but to stay there himself until he received letters. He telegraphed back to say that Barri was ill, and that he disliked to move him; still, he made an effort to do so, but found that the boy was too unwell to travel.

Barri was, undoubtedly, very ill. He had Mediterranean fever. 'A matter,' said the most excellent doctor, 'which time alone can remedy, Mr. Drummond. You are, I think, the now celebrated Mr. Drummond, of whom the lady, Carlina, forsooth, has written to me!'

'I am at a loss to understand what you mean, doctor.'

'It will be, I suppose, in the Courts of Law; so, why need we avoid speaking of it? It is a simple thing, and often happens here, as, probably, in respectable England. Madame Arnaud came here with her child. Drummond also came here with Mrs. Arnaud. He desired that her child should be taken from her. He was legal adviser of Lord — the English names are droll.'

'Festiniog?'

'Exactly. Well, why more? Carlina and her relations did the matter for Drummond, and was, no doubt, paid. Her family assisted her; she has now telegraphed to her family to tell the whole truth about the matter. They will probably do so, if they are paid. I have known it for years; but what business could it be of mine? It remains, beyond doubt, that you are the cousin of this boy.'

'I cannot believe it.'

'Well, that is your affair. Half Ravenna will swear to it. The lawyer, Drummond, managed the business, and he will have to manage very dexterously to get out of the difficulty. The woman, Carlina, has paid her relations to keep this thing quiet; now, she has sent a message to say that she has made another bargain, and that the truth is to be told. You have, as far as I understand, only this boy between you and a vast fortune.'

'I will accept that as truth,' said George Drummond. 'Is the boy very ill?'

'He might live, or, with care, might die!'

'And no one the wiser, doctor?'

'No.'

'How well you speak English!' said George Drummond.

'I have practised much in Rome,' said the doctor.

'What should be done with him, if you wished him to live?' said George Drummond.

'He should be kept warm, he should have some one in bed with him. That is our practice.'

'And if you wanted him to die?'

'Well, if he is kept low and cold, a boy of that age would die. If you want to keep him alive, give him beef-tea and stimulants every four hours. If you want him to die, leave him alone. That is all I have to say. But I warn you, Mr. Drummond, that it is a very dangerous thing to go very near him and take his breath. Our fever is most distinctly contagious.'

'But, under the circumstances which you mention, the boy may live?'

'Undoubtedly. I will call to-morrow morning.' And so, the doctor went away.

The object of the death of Barri was now fully understood by George Drummond. He was next in succession. Lord Festiniog was too old to marry. Lady Rhyader could never have any more children, and he would be an Earl with 50,000*l.* a year. It was time for him to act in the matter.

He went to Barri's bedside. The boy was getting delirious, and his breath came hot, foul, and poisonous. He propped his head up and wiped his lips. The doctor had said that he was to have port wine and beef—where were they to be got? Not even at the British Consul's, at that hour.

But there was brandy and some portable soup which they had bought on their travels. He made a mixture of these things, and got the boy to swallow them. Then, he turned the silly old crone who was watching the boy, out of the room, telling her that he was going to sleep with him. She went, saying that he was going to his death-bed. She had never learnt the magnificence of duty. In what school could she possibly have been taught it?

The boy turned, sometimes, in the night, with his fœtid breath hot on George's cheek: he asked always for drink, and George got up and gave it to him, though one act of neglect on his part might have given him all that he desired in this world.

Mrs. Arnaud who scarcely cared for him, Lord Festiniog who scarcely liked him, Lord Rhyader who did not care to think about him, would have held different opinions about him, had they seen his patient love for the boy who stood between him and all his earthly ambition, through the next three days. The only man who really loved him, the only man who would have understood him, the only man who ever knew him at his best, was the poor, ruined, maddened attorney, Drummond, whom he had so long believed to be his father.

On the morning of the second day, he made enquiries, about Ravenna, as to the circumstances made known to him by the doctor. There was no doubt about them. The good folks of Ravenna laughed when they were spoken to on the subject. On the third day he got a letter from Lord Festiniog, saying that he was *primâ facie* satisfied, and commending Barri to his care.

So, the poor wearied head of Barri rolled about upon the pillow, and George Drummond watched it, as though it was the most precious thing to him in the world. One single act of neglect would have put him in a splendid position, and given him everything which the world could give.

But George Drummond was a better nurse to the boy than could have been got for money. Why? Simply, because he loved the boy better than he did himself: and because, prig as he was, he loved his duty better than either.

CHAPTER V.

A DISASTER.

By degrees, his charge recovered, and George gladly obeyed orders from home to return. The time selected was long past the equinox, and it seemed hard to go from the bright Italian sky into the darkness of London. They went again to Rome, and, by medical advice, stayed there a short time, and saw the Pope again: which was, at once, a mystery and a delight to Barri. George was a Protestant, and tried to teach the boy that the present Pope, though the most amiable of mankind, was, personally and authoritatively, the enemy of all that was good. It was no use at all, the traditions of his family were too strong; his ancestor De Barri, Giraldus Cambrensis, had admired the Popes of those times, why should not he admire the Pope of these times? George had no answer to his young charge, and they got on very admirably until they came wandering to Leghorn.

Here, Barri was slightly ill again, and George got alarmed about him. He sent for the famous English doctor there, and consulted him.

The doctor said that Barri had a slight relapse, and ought to be kept perfectly quiet with as little motion as possible.

'But,' said George, 'I am his tutor, and I am ordered to bring him home; the boy is heir to a large estate, and I dare not show my face in England if anything happened to him.'

'I should not take him over the Alps,' said the doctor. 'Does he mind the sea?'

'Not at all.'

'Then, take him round by steamer, and let him get the fresh air: it would be the best thing in the world for the boy.'

'There is no danger at this time of the year?' said George.

'Good heavens! my dear sir, we are not in the North sea. *We* never have *our* ships lost, even in the Bay of Biscay. No, take your pupil round by sea by all means. But I see that you are in difficulty; who is your patron?'

'Lord Festiniog.'

'He is head of the family still, eh?'

'Yes, and likely to remain so.'

'Well, then,' said the doctor, 'I will write to him and tell him, that you, as tutor, did not recommend the course, but that it was done on my authority.'

'I shall be much obliged to you,' said George, and the Doctor wrote.

'My Lord,—I have ordered, on my professional responsibility, that Mr. Barri Arnaud, the hope of your house, should not cross the Alps at this late season. Mr. Drummond, his respectable and intelligent tutor, will, therefore, take him by sea from this place.

'The boy requires quinine and iron; also, I should let him have port wine in your climate, not, of course, in sufficient quantities to encourage a desire for stimulants, but in sufficient quantity. Exercise, change of scene, and athletics, but not objectless ones, are what the boy mostly wants. Expand his chest or he will never make an orator the thing, I suppose, which you desire.

'As for yourself, don't believe in colchicum for that gout of yours. Come here, and I will get you up in a fortnight. Climate, my dear lord, climate is everything, and there is no climate in the world like Leghorn. To me it was left to discover this city.

'Your Humble Servant,

'GEORGE PILGARLIC, M.D.'

'Shall I send this by post, or will you enclose it to Lord Festiniog?' said the doctor.

'I will enclose it,' said George Drummond.

'Good, then, here it is: I will introduce to the Captain of the *Newcastle*, and see that you have the best berths. What is this I see? My dear sir, I never take fees from people in Lord Festiniog's position, it does not pay in the long run—I mean that I am already under too deep obligations to his lordship.

George Drummond wrote to Lord Festiniog, and told him of the decision. He enclosed another letter, strangely different from the doctor's.

'Sir,—As you now know the whole facts of your position, I can be perfectly frank with you. When this letter is gone to you, I shall show a copy of it to my lord; not before Mr. Drummond has left London, and has gone south, with what purpose I am not prepared to say. I only say that two courses are open to you.

'If you bring the boy Barri over the Alps, there is great danger to him. I should not do that if I were in your place. I think it dangerous. I know it to be dangerous.

I, most certainly, if I cared for his life, should do nothing of the kind.

'A sea-voyage after our marsh fever is always recommended. By avoiding the Alps and coming by sea from any port, you would save two people from the commission of a crime, yourself, and Mr. Drummond.

'CARLINA GERSOTTI.'

George Drummond thanked God that the difficulty was cleared out of his way by the independent testimony of two people. He would get his cousin home, and remove the horrible responsibility from his shoulders. The boy, whose death would ennoble him, was getting dearer and dearer to him.

And he saw such wondrous promise in the boy; Barri had twice the intelligence which he had had at the same age, and only wanted education: that he could give, and make a great man of him, as he thought. 'I shall see him from afar off at first, but the deuce is in it if I don't make a name in the world too: I in one place, he in another. We shall make a sound in both houses yet.'

So they sped away across the Mediterranean. What were his thoughts about the man who had been such a kind father to him? We cannot say. All we know of the man is from Barri, and to Barri he never mentioned Mr. Drummond or Mrs. Arnaud. The boy was in absolute ignorance, to the last, that George was his cousin. That had been agreed on between Lord Festiniog and himself: the boy was only to know after they came home. And so they went on their voyage together, Barri looking about the ship, and George watching him, as though the slightest accident would not put him in a position for which some men would have committed a crime.

The bay was passed and they saw Ushant under a lurid sunset. The barometer had lowered so suddenly that the captain made up all his fires and headed apparently for America. George laughed to him about his course.

'If we get behind the Start, Mr. Drummond,' he said, 'we are lucky. You are no sailor.'

'Why, no,' said George Drummond, 'will there be any danger?'

'God knows,' said the captain, 'the ship is too long and too narrow. By Jove! see, there it comes.'

The sun had scarcely sunk into the sea, when the western sky was as black as pitch. As sail after sail which it was impossible to get in, was blown away, with a sound like a cannon followed by a rattle of musketry, George Drummond stood on deck, amused with his good fortune in seeing a real storm at sea. He went down once to where Barri was now sleeping quietly, and looked at him. He had no thought of danger, but the boy seemed cold, and he put another coat over him ; then, he went on deck.

It was piercing cold, and the engine room looked bright and warm. There had been a heavy Atlantic sea all day, necessitating the using of the compensating gear, for her screw was frequently out of water. He was a great friend of the engineer, and he stepped down, cigar in mouth, to see how the gear worked. He sat in the little room and baked himself. The engineer was not at all alarmed: though, as the captain had put her head, she was pitching heavily.

It was beautiful to sit in the warmth,

and watch the working of the compensation gear: as her bow dipped it spun rapidly, as her stern dropped it stopped slowly: they have better things of the kind now, but the original one was a splendid idea.

Her stern was out of the water higher than ever, and they were nearly unseated. The compensation gear was spinning as hard as ever: it had got out of order. The engineer rose hurriedly, with an oath, but it was too late, a ripping crack went through the ship, hurried feet were heard overhead, and the word went about that the screw shaft was broken.

At once, of course, the ship was in the trough of the sea, a more fearfully dangerous engine of destruction than Mr. Victor Hugo's celebrated loose cannon. Every mast went overboard directly, at her first whip up into the wind. She was nothing better than a floating wreck, with the sea bursting on board of her every moment. In ten minutes, the warm engine room was changed into a sea of stinking steam, in ten minutes more, it was a seething sea of black coal mud.

George hurried to Barri at once. He had been thrown out of his bunk, and was dressing himself. He took him up to the cabin, and, then, he asked what was the matter.

'There is danger. Will you sit here while I go down again?'

'I will try to stand,' said Barri.

George was scarcely away from him for five minutes, then, he came up with his desk, and wrote a few hurried words, which he folded up and put in the breast pocket of Barri's pea jacket.

'We might part, Barri, you see,' he said. 'Give that note to Lord Festiniog. You must get ready, my boy, I hear the captain ordering out the boats.'

Barri was perfectly still, but very much frightened. The captain came in, hurriedly, after a time, and said: 'Mr. Drummond, I have lost my ship; I have the long boat out and some men in her, will you and your charge jump into her at once, or she will be stove against the side?'

'Now, Barri, be firm,' said George. 'You must leap into the boat.' And so they passed out of the cabin into the horrible hell of the tempest.

The ship was begining to settle down. One boat had been got out, and she was still fast to the ship. George put Barri on the bulwarks, and told him to jump into her. The boy was terrified.

A brave man might have been. The boat was surging, leaping, diving nearly head under, in the lee of the ship, at one time near the side, at another an oar's length away. The men in her were shouting to those who were on the bulwarks to leap: few dared; was the boy to blame?

'Leap yourself, Mr. Drummond,' said the captain; 'the men will cut the painter directly, your life is more valuable than the boy's.'

George Drummond had other ideas, though; he took Barri in his arms, and at the next and last surge of the boat towards the ship he dropped the boy among the sailors at his feet, before she swerved away from the ship again. The man at the bow cut the painter, and the boat parted from the ship. A great roller parted them, and they saw one another no more.

CHAPTER VI.

BARRI'S RETURN.

Lord Rhyader received, one morning, the following singular telegram:

'Brown Jones, Falmouth. Lord Rhyader, Bolton Street, Piccadilly. 'Come here at once. Boat "Nemesis" has been picked up by "Arethusa," and men landed here in Sailors' Home. Boy says that he is your son: men confirm it. Boy rather exhausted. Come directly.'

Lord Rhyader had for some time disliked to do anything without his father's advice or knowledge. The fact was that

Lady Rhyader was getting a little peevish, and they did not get on so well together as they did formerly. She always, when consulted about anything, at once opposed it, without a moment's thought, and then defended her opinion through thick and thin, while, on the other hand, old Lord Festiniog always thought before he spoke, and then gave the best advice he could. Consequently he gained, without meaning it, a power over Rhyader which his wife had lost. She knew it, and was jealous of it. Lord and Lady Rhyader were, of course, on the best of terms, but it was impossible to deny that there was not more confidence between father and son, than between wife and husband. He, on this occasion, however, never thought for one instant of his father; with an energy of tenderness which he had not shown for a few years, he ran into her dressing-room, and, with his arm round her neck, read the message to her.

'Alice,' he said, 'you must help me now.'

'Gervase,' she replied, 'I am as well able to help you as Lord Festiniog: or, indeed, as Mary Arnaud. We must act together here, my love, and never act apart any more.'

Lord Rhyader was man enough to say no more: if she had been in the wrong, so had he. They had both been a little too much absorbed in their separate selves, and the potential disaster united them at once. The truth must be told, they had never cared very greatly for the boy: he did not suit them, and they were more comfortable without him than with him. Now, however, he was likely to be lost by some hitherto unexplained disaster, they were in confidence instantly: in a confidence which lasted to their deaths—as far as it went.

They both knew that their mutual confidence had returned. They made no effort at an explanation, the chances would have been as ten to one that they would have quarrelled had they done so. The new, unspoken reconciliation between them was so pleasant that neither of them desired words.'

'We must start at once, Gervase,' she said, with a view of bringing in other matters.

'At once,' he said, ringing the bell, which was answered before either of them spoke. He and she gave directions for an immediate and sudden journey, and they were alone again. She chivalrously broke the ice for him.

'This is a piece of your father's work, Gervase.'

'So it seems,' said Lord Rhyader.

'Our boy Barri is sent abroad with George Drummond, who it seems is heir to the house. Do you believe it?'

'Yes, darling. I think that there is little doubt about it. Don't attempt to dispute that. Drummond has confessed it, you know.'

'Well, I will not dispute it. But that young man is suddenly taken into favour, and sent abroad with our boy. Who did that? answer me.'

'My father.'

'Exactly. And what do you think of your father now?' This was said with scorn.

Lord Rhyader thought about his father as he had always done, as a good gentleman and a kind friend. But he saw from Lady Rhyader's eyes that she considered that she had scored a point against him, and was too polite to contradict her. He said nothing, but looked as if there was really nothing to be said in palliation of his father.

'Mark my words, Gervase,' she said solemnly, rising up to prepare for her journey, 'this is a plot, hatched out at No. 17, and Mary Arnaud is in it. Your father, although dictatorial, is weak, and he has been led into it by that woman.'

'But, my dearest Alice, I don't think——'

'Good. When I am dead, and you know the truth, you will remember my words. I will go and get ready for my journey.'

'But, Alice, my father would not lend himself to anything underhand. You must think of that.'

She thought of it, at once, in her usual way, for one second, and then enlarged upon it, without exactly knowing what she was going to say next. 'You will find it, Gervase, exactly as I have put it to you: and if your father was here before me, I would tell him the same thing. Will you be convinced by one question? Where is George Arnaud?'

Lord Rhyader seemed to think that there was a great deal in that, though he could not tell why, knowing nothing about the matter. He said, rather meekly, 'I suppose we had better send this telegram on to my father?'

'I suppose that you had better,' she said: 'that would be only decent; but let us get to Falmouth first. I don't want his interference.'

They were a difficult couple to move. The telegram had been sent to Lord Festiniog more than two hours before they were at Paddington. They were not deeply anxious, for there was nothing to make them so in the telegram. They took the journey quite comfortably in the train at noon, wrapping themselves up warm, eating and drinking, in a trifling manner, and getting up their mutual case against Lord Festiniog. Lady Rhyader acted as attorney, and Rhyader himself accepted the brief provisionally, knowing perfectly well that he would no more dare to say one half of the things to his father which his wife put into his mouth than he dared fly. However, he knew that his father had some sixty or eighty thousand pounds which he could leave to his groom, and so he held a large trump card over his wife, in case she should go too far, and provoke an entire rupture. He let her ease her long suppressed mind on Lord Festiniog, therefore, with the greatest complacency: and they got on most charmingly: particularly as he intended to make her spokeswoman in the business, whatever it was. And that he could not quite make out; there was to be a war of liberation from his father's authority, and his father in his chivalry would never quarrel with him for taking his wife's part. If there was to be any real fighting, she could do it better than he could; and he could always check her by reminding her of the loose cash.

So they amiably got to Shrivenham, and got out there to walk about while the train was being shunted. It was an unusual thing and Lord Rhyader asked the station-master the reason of it.

'A special train a-coming through, sir. Stand back there! stand back!'

A distant humming sound, then a long-drawn shriek; then an approaching roar which swelled upon the ear. Then a vision of a fiery dragon filled with smoke, fire, and steam, coming towards them swifter than the wind, with pulses going quicker than a madman's heart; how smoke-grimed, stedfast men upon the monster's back, guiding it as it shook the station with a shock like an earthquake. One saloon carriage in the rear of the engine, which seemed to leap at the point. That was all, the whole terrible and dangerous arrangement was out of sight before the echoes which it had raised could die away.

Lord and Lady Rhyader continued their journey methodically. The greatest event in their journey to Falmouth was that Lady Rhyader's maid lost a shawl. The loss was discovered at Exeter; the lady's maid having, as a preliminary to confession, given a month's warning in the waiting-room, told Lady

Rhyader of the awful fact. Lady Rhyader was in tears at once. It was not a very valuable shawl, and she could not bear to part with her maid. She did not care about the matter, and Rhyader with that shrewdness which his father ranked so high, discovered that the maid had got the shawl on herself: and the valet proved that in the confusion at Shrivenham he had, in an absent moment, put it over the young woman's shoulders. Lady Rhyader made her a present of the shawl, and so sold her liberty to her maid. The month's notice was withdrawn, and they, to use a Devonshire expression, drumbled on to Falmouth.

What was their astonishment when they were met by Lord Festiniog at the door of the hotel! He was among a group of sailors, talking eagerly to them, but he seemed to know of the Rhyaders' coming perfectly well, and to take little thought about it.

'I have got the boy here, upstairs,' he said; 'but I doubt if we shall ever make anything of him again. It is the most unhappy business which ever was seen. The poor boy is idiotic. I can't get anything out of him. He has had a shock to the system from which he will never recover, unless we take very great care of him.'

Lady Rhyader, now, was seriously alarmed. Her rebellion against Lord Festiniog might stand over, at all events for a time. She went swiftly upstairs to Barri, and from the moment she saw him never thought about herself as long as she lived. After she had once seen the boy she thought no more of Lord Festiniog. The terror of the sight before her put every frivolous and ill-tempered idea from her mind for ever. Who was to blame for the catastrophe? She cared nothing at all. It was her own child who was before her, the child for whom she had cared too little, as she saw now, but, in what fearful case!

Worn almost to a skeleton, he was sitting up in bed, rocking his body to and fro, as if to allow for the motion of a boat. His right hand, thin with illness, clutched the mattress convulsively, while his left was held up as if to shield him from an enemy expected every moment. The nurse explained it to her. The boy had been three days in the open boat in the heavy sea, and had sat like that with his right hand clasping the gunwale, trying to shield himself from the drenching waves which sometimes broke over them from the South West. 'The men put him to leeward, ma'amn,' said the nurse; 'that is why he holds his left arm up to shield himself, and holds on to the gunwale with the other.'

'Why will not he lie down?' said Lady Rhyader, utterly terrified.

'He will never lie down any more, Ma'am,' said the nurse. 'He will have the rattles in the throat in ten minutes.'

'Get out you old fool, do,' said a voice behind them. 'How dare you, you crone, frighten her ladyship like this, when you know that the best man in Europe has given his opinion to-day?'

Lady Rhyader turned: it was Lord Festiniog who spoke.

'My dear Alice,' he said, 'do not listen to the croaking of this old witch. When you sent me the telegram this morning, I did two things,—ordered a special train, and got Sir Alexander McFittie to come with me. He says that the boy will not die, but that he has a nervous shock which will spoil his career, at least for a very long time. You must brace up your nerves, my dear, you must nurse the boy, and so make him fonder of you than he was before. That is easily done, for he is an affectionate little fellow, and you might make him, at least, as fond of you as he is of me.'

He was going to say,—as he was of Mary Arnaud—but he thought twice before he said that.

'Lady Rhyader,' he said, suddenly and sternly.

'Yes, Lord Festiniog.'

'Have you done your duty by this boy?'

'No,' she said. 'You always made the boy jealous of us. How could we possibly do our duty by him?'

Lord Festiniog had never looked on it in that light before. He said:—

'I should not have looked on the matter in that light myself.'

'Without doubt,' said Lady Rhyader, determined to win every point she could possibly score, but wondering what would be the next one.

'Well, let bygones be bygones, let us take care of the boy. You stay with him, I must go and break the news to Mary Arnaud.' And so he went out to Lord Rhyader, leaving mother and son together.

'What, on earth, has Mary Arnaud got to do with it?' thought Lady Rhyader. But there was the boy, delirious in his bed, calling out for that woman and not for his own mother.

CHAPTER VII.

THE VANITY OF HUMAN WISHES.

HE found Lord Rhyader alone, walking up and down the room, and a very important conversation ensued between them.

'I have made light of your boy's case to Alice, Gervase,' he said, 'but there is no doubt whatever that he is extremely ill, and it is very doubtful if he will live to be a man. You must really rouse yourself to look facts in the face. The boy has undergone horrors and privations which have half killed those strong sailors who have brought him home. Do you know that a mutinous part of the boat's crew wanted to ——'

'Well?'

'Well,—wanted to kill the boy for a horrible purpose. It was only by the resolution of two or three that he was saved. And he knew it, for he heard them talking about it, and he will, it is feared, never get it out of his head any more; such shocks are not felt at his time of life without permanent results.'

'I am deeply grieved, father, but I do not share your fears to this extent which you speak of. I cannot understand your anxiety.'

'It is real, however,' said Lord Festiniog. 'I loved the boy, I think, better than you did.'

'I will not argue that point, father,' said Gervase. 'If you loved him so much, why did you insist on his going abroad with his only rival?'

'I sent him abroad to keep him out of mischief. I sent him abroad with George Arnaud because I trusted the young man. He has gloriously fulfilled his trust.'

'By bringing back my boy an idiot,' said Lord Rhyader.'

'Bringing?'

'Yes. I suppose he has taken care of himself?'

'George! Have you not heard? George went down with the ship, and saved the boy at the sacrifice of his own life!'

'Good heavens!'

Lord Rhyader was silent for some time He was a just man, and his regret at having been so unjust to George was great. 'You are sure of this,' he said.

'Hear for yourself; ask one of the sailors in. Send in George Horrocks,' he said to a waiter who was in the room.

A sailor came in. 'My son, Lord Rhyader,' said Lord Festiniog, 'wishes to ask you a question or two. Your general evidence will be given before the Board, of course, but answer him what he asks you.'

'I wanted to know if Mr. Drummond could have saved his own life, if he had deserted the boy whom he dropped into the boat?'

'Most certainly, sir,' said the sailor: 'half-a-dozen times over. The boy was frightened and would not jump, and so, he gave up his own life for the boy's, fair and square. No doubt about *that.*'

'And you saw him drowned after, with no attempt to save him?'

'We had done all that it was possible for men to do. We kept near her until she went down, in hopes that some one might rise, but I need hardly say that no one did.

We incurred great danger by not keeping the boat's head straight before the wind, at once, as you would know, my lord, if you were a sailor.'

'I beg your pardon,' said Lord Rhyader. 'I have no doubt that everything was done. 'I wish you a good afternoon,' and the man went.

'There is the end,' said Lord Festiniog; 'the end of a good family, too.'

'If Barri dies.'

'Well, his life is very problematical. In case of his death, the entailed property all goes to you, and, I suppose, afterwards to some religious establishment. I am more sorry than ever about George.'

'You seem to think more of him than you do of Barri, now.'

'There you do me an injustice, as usual, Rhyader. I have a stronger personal feeling for the boy than ever I had for poor George Arnaud. I loved the boy better than ever you did. My feeling for him is one thing, my feeling for the extinction of our family is another.'

'The remedy lies entirely in your own hands, father,' said Rhyader. 'Alice will live to any age and have no more children. The remedy lies with yourself.'

'I do not see how.'

'Marry, yourself.'

Lord Festiniog kept steady on his feet, but, morally, he reeled as this proposition was made to him. He had not thought of such a thing for thirty years. Was Rhyader mad?

Apparently not. He was most perfectly cool over the matter, and appeared in earnest. He repeated:

'Marry, yourself.'

'But you would not approve *that*,' said Lord Festiniog.

'I should, most entirely,' said Lord Rhyader. 'Why should I not? It can make no difference to me, and would prevent my feeling any responsibility as to the disposal of the property.'

'But I am so old,' said Lord Festiniog, still doubting if he heard aright.

'Not a bit. You are only sixty-two.'

'But whom am I to marry? You are mad. Have you any one in your eye? Have you ever thought of this before?'

'Never. It only came into my head when I heard your description of poor Barri. As for the lady, why, you must choose for yourself; I really am too much out of the world to advise you.'

'Just conceive how very much at random you are talking, my dear Rhyader.

What would Alice say to you, if she knew that you had made this proposition?'

'Oh! you must not think of speaking about it to her yet. It may come to nothing. Think about it for yourself.'

'Lord Festiniog had plenty of time to think about it, for he by no means went back by express. The slowest train on the line would do for him *now*, for at the other end he had to tell poor Mary Arnaud that her newly-found and scarcely-known son was dead.

'Poor thing!' he said to himself. 'This world is very hard on her. There seems to be no end to her troubles. I wish she could have made up her mind to marry Drummond, and that he had not been such a rascal. She might have been happy with him.'

He had forgotten the awful proposal

which Lord Rhyader had made, of his own marriage. This thought of Mrs. Arnaud's marriage brought it back to him with a shock.

Going by a slow train, Lord Festiniog naturally met with an accident. His own special train, in which he had come down, had to be sent back to Paddington somehow. It was sent back in the rear of the ordinary slow train, and, by way of distinguishing *itself*, dashed into the ordinary train by a combination of circumstances which were afterwards proved to be entirely impossible. It was clearly proved before the Board of Trade that the thing never could have happened, and yet it did, for all that, and Lord Festiniog broke one of the small bones in his hand, and in trying to give assistance had his whiskers scorched by the fire of one of the engines. When asked which, he declined to answer the question as he might commit the company, in which he was a large shareholder.

He, however, got to London somehow, and was driven to his house in due time. To his great surprise he found that Mr. Drummond had called three times on that morning. He had not thought that Drummond would have sought him so very eagerly, and he was puzzled.

Meanwhile, it was necessary, in common kindness, for him to go and see Mary Arnaud, and break the news to her as gently as possible. He had not been near No. 17 for some time, and felt considerably guilty on that score. Mary, of whom he was secretly afraid, would be angry with him in the first instance. She had always had a good case against the family, and now had a stronger one. He would have to tell her that her so recently acknowledged son was drowned. It was not a very agreeable matter under any circumstances: still less so under the present.

People enjoy themselves in three ways: by anticipation of a pleasure, by the realisation of that pleasure, and by the recollection of it afterwards. In the same way people plague themselves in three ways: by the anticipation of the trouble, by the realisation of the trouble (which is generally not half what they thought it to be), and thirdly by the solution of the trouble, and the humiliating doubt as to whether there was any trouble to be afraid of after all.

Lord Festiniog was deeply plagued about Mary. He knew, or thought that he knew, that he should have a scene with her. And he was not well, the railway accident had shaken him, his finger was in pain, and that irritated him. He had anticipated more than half his troubles, however, before he drove up to her door, at nine o'clock in the evening.

The house was completely dark, as he knocked at the private door. It was opened with startling rapidity, and he found himself pulled into the passage, and the door shut behind him. There being no light, he was unaware of what was going to happen to him; he was not long in doubt. He was kissed in the dark all over his face.

'Darling,' said the kisser, 'it is so good of you to come from the club so soon; and you have not been smoking. Good child, come up now and smoke in our bedroom.'

The lady, who had her arm round his neck, was proceeding to stroke his hair. Lord Festiniog had gone as far in an explanatory speech as, 'Madam, I think you are in error,' when the hall was suddenly illuminated by two candles. Lord Festiniog saw that one of them was carried by Mrs. Arnaud, and the other by the terrible old madame of Paris. Regarding himself as a lost man, he looked down to see who was accidentally kissing him. He discovered at once that it was ex-Mademoiselle Heloise, now Mrs. D'Arcy.

She, with a shriek which was nearly a yell, fled for protection to her grandmother, and threw herself on her bosom. They both came down together; Madame Mantalent, being underneath, made some vigorous attempts to break her granddaughter's head with the candlestick. Mrs. D'Arcy, now alive to the situation, and having had to do the thing once or twice before, defended herself in such a scientific manner, that Madame Mantalent cast the candlestick at

Lord Festiniog, and begged for life, saying that she was an old woman, and would not trouble them long.

Lord Festiniog and Mary Arnaud got the old lady on her feet, and took her into the little parlour. Mrs. D'Arcy, the gentle and excellent Heloise, came into them, and, then, it appeared that that most excellent of young ladies had lost her temper.

She was as beautiful as ever; nay, she was looking better than ever she had done; but old Lord Festiniog's eyes were opened, as regarded her, for the first time. The thin crust of *bourgeois* French respectability had been worn through, and the real nature appeared below.

Let us not be misunderstood in any way. Three-quarters of France, and three-quarters of Ireland produce a population which the whole world, for certain qualities, cannot match. But there is a residuum in both countries unmanageable, and save on one solitary subject, unsympathetic. We name no provinces in either kingdom, and yet we know that we have to deal with certain people, possessing certain virtues, as we would with wild beasts.

Heloise came from a part of France pre-eminent for its virtues, but also pre-eminent for its temper. She had lost her temper, firstly, because she had kissed Lord Festiniog in the dark, and secondly, because her grandmother, who came from the same part of the country, had beaten her over the head with the candlestick. What is mainly to the purpose, however, is the fact that the scene which followed between her and her mother, put the idea of matrimony in a rather difficult light to Lord Festiniog's eyes.

The debate was carried on in the French language, which was possibly a relief to the servants, but none to Mrs. Arnaud or Lord Festiniog, who were both mistress and master of that fluent and elegant language, so well adapted for all phases of soul. Mrs. D'Arcy and Madame Mantalent being both extremely angry, used the resources at their command with all the genius of their nation. At one period of her life, Madame Mantalent had not been so successful in her affairs as she was now, and every detail of those times was hurled in her teeth with the most singular epithets. In this 'hurling in the teeth,' the fact that those teeth were false, and that they never had been paid for until the outraged laws of France forced the old lady to do so, was by no means forgotten. Madame Mantalent's establishment also was, as we have previously said, a place of meeting for innocent lovers: this circumstance was now turned against the old Lady with singular *esprit.* Some of the marriages, practically, made up in the *magazine*, had by no means turned out so well as those which are proverbially made in heaven; and the details of many of them were alluded to by Mrs. D'Arcy, not only with singular freedom, but with powers of oratory which excited the surprise, almost the admiration, of Lord Festiniog. In fact, that most admirable and gentle housewife, Mrs. D'Arcy, ended, as his lordship afterwards rudely expressed himself to Lord Rhyader, without a single rag of character to cover her back. One transaction, involving 25,000 francs, a penniless duke in the employment of the later empire, and a young heiress, was so repeatedly alluded to that Lord Festiniog lost the thread of the story in consequence of Mrs. D'Arcy's volubility, and he could not quite make out whether it was the wife who had exchanged into a regiment of turco for service in Algeria, or whether it was the husband who had burned men. It was made perfectly certain, however, by this young lady that they both cursed the day on which they saw Madame Mantalent.

Madame, however, seated now peacefully in Mrs. Arnaud's easy chair, with a glass of curaçoa, let her granddaughter scold herself into quiescence, without doing anything but agreeing with a sardonic laugh to everything which the young lady said; occasionally, correcting her when she appeared to soften circumstances, and saying, '*bon! bon!*' when she made a more desperately ruinous assault on her reputation. Scolding cannot last for ever, as both ladies knew perfectly well; and Madame Mantalent, with the military genius of her nation, allowed her enemy to exhaust her resources, before she attacked her in full force. Nay, she showed more than the usual military genius of the nation, great as it is: she combined it with that of such great generals as Fabius Cunctator, Frederick the Great, the Duke of Wellington in the last Spanish campaign, and General Grant in his advance upon Richmond. She chose her own time of fighting, the neglect of which rule has ruined both the Napoleons.

When Mrs. D'Arcy was quite exhausted, it became her turn to receive punishment, and by this time, her husband was in the room, wondering what could possibly be the matter. The old lady had calculated on this with the subtlety of a Cleopatra, or a Catherine de' Medici. In the most inexorable manner she overhauled the character of

Heloise before her bridegroom, in a way which made Lord Festiniog desire to kill her. Heloise had been, in her way, a very considerable flirt, and had drawn a very great deal of money into the perfectly virtuous establishment of her grandmother without receiving any recognisable percentage on the same. Still, she was a good girl, as her grandmother perfectly well knew. Every man she had spoken to as a friend was now made out to be a lover, and the old lady absolutely revelled in the disclosures which she thought she was making before a jealous English husband. The end was that Mrs. D'Arcy was reduced to somewhat spiteful tears.

It was becoming very distressing until D'Arcy came forward to his wife, and kissing her kindly, burst into a laugh. 'She says, in effect, that the men all ran after you,' he said, 'of course they did, I did, and, what is more, I have got you. Ah madame, you can't prevent that!'

'You have got a fickle heart and a bad temper, Mr. D'Arcy,' said the old lady. But D'Arcy only laughed at her and went away pleasantly with Heloise.

'Good evening, madame,' said Lord Festiniog. 'Mary, you must come up stairs with me at once, I have something to say to you which can wait no longer, though I wish that some other cause of delay would intervene before I tell it to you.'

'Come, then,' she said, leading the way, here are the bride and bridegroom toiling up-stairs before us. Say a good word to them, as few, except you, can say it.'

'But it would be a liberty.'

'Not in the case of an old man like you,' she said, 'you can say anything.'

'Anything,' he thought, 'but what have come to say. This horrible procrastination!'

He ran up-stairs and touched D'Arcy's arm. 'Captain D'Arcy,' he said, touching his arm, 'I hope you will allow a very old man, like myself, to tell you, before your wife, that you have behaved like a most loyal gentleman, in not paying attention to Madame Mantalent's objurgations.'

D'Arcy looked at him in calm wonder.

'Did you think such a thing possible, then, Lord Festiniog?'

'I could not say. I hope that I have not taken a liberty. But you behaved so very well, that, as an old man, I thought I might speak.'

'I am only too proud of your approval, but, indeed, I saw this little woman of mine in Paris under such difficult circumstances and temptations, that nothing would shake my faith in her now; not even Madame Mantalent's tongue.'

Lord Festiniog admired the young man's chivalry, and bade him good-night. From certain things which madame had let drop, 'let drop,'—we say—poured out in buckets, he rather thought that his imperfect acquaintance with the French tongue, when spoken with extreme volubility and with a pure Parisian accent, had something to do with his complacence. However, here was Mary following up-stairs; here was her room, and here was —— sitting in her chair, another Heloise, much older than Mrs. D'Arcy, and, in his opinion, considerably more beautiful.

'Oh, you are here, Clotilde, my dear soul. Grandma and Heloise have been quarrelling down-stairs. Lord Festiniog, this is my cousin, Mademoiselle Clotilde Aubignè. Try to make friends with her, for she has been a loving friend to me.'

'Say no more, Mary, say no more,' said Lord Festiniog. 'We want a mutual friend to-night; I hope that Mademoiselle Clotilde will let me number her among mine.'

As she advanced towards him, offering her hand; as he looked at her matured, Madonna like beauty—so like that of Heloise in feature and colouring, and so unlike it in its splendid repose—Lord Festiniog found a little monitor in his left breast, asking him if he was quite so old as he had represented himself to the D'Arcys, on the stairs. Was that admiration for him, in her eyes? 'No, I am not vain enough for that at my time of life,' he said, 'It is only the reflection of my own admiration in hers.'

'Can this lady in whom you have, as you say, the most entire confidence, stay with us while I tell you some very distressing news?'

'Yes, I would rather she did. God has sent her to me as a comfort, and why should she leave me? Clotilde you will stay, will you not? Now, my dear papa, what makes you so grave?'

'Mary, you are a widow.'

'Yes,' she said, with a sudden movement of her hands.

'You are now a childless one.'

She looked at him steadily, and said:—

'I do not understand you.'

'Your son George is drowned.'

'When I was trying to love him—when I was hoping, hoping for his return—when I was thinking of every good quality which his father possessed, and endeavouring to see them reflected in him? This is rather hard, is it not? It is cruel.'

'The sea is very cruel, Mary.'

'Ay! but God is more cruel than the sea itself. I was not prepared for this. Let me be quiet awhile. I would rather that no one spoke to me for a short time, if they did not mind.'

She bent her head over the fire, and Clotilde beckoned to Lord Festiniog to come and sit beside her. He went to her, and she took his hand in hers, while she whispered in French:—'Good and admirable friend, what has happened?'

'Her son is drowned,' said Lord Festiniog. 'Drowned in the most noble manner, but at the bottom of the deep sea for all that. She will wish to know the particulars immediately. Stay with us, dear lady, while I tell them to her.'

He took her hand, and kissed it.

'I will stay with you by all means, my lord,' she said, 'but she will want an answer soon. She was getting to love the son so little known to her. Yes, my lord, she will be wanting an explanation soon, and I will stay with you. She has never said anything but good about you.'

Mrs. Arnaud rose and confronted them at this point. She was not in the least degree angry or *emportée* but she was terrible in her beauty for all that. Lord Festiniog was glad that he had such a protection in the gentle, though unknown, Clotilde, against the equally gentle, though better known, Mary.

'Lord Festiniog,' she said, 'I wish to say a few words. Did I ever seek an alliance with your house?'

'Certainly not, Mary.'

'Did I ever seek to intrude myself on you, until after I had discovered that I was legally married?'

'Certainly not, Mary. But you must remember ——'

'I know. You and Rhyader were kind, believing me not to be legally married. When you could dispute the fact no longer, what did you do?'

'Acknowledged the fact, Mary, you cannot deny *that*.'

'Yes, after you were forced to do so. Drummond did that for me. I owe more to Drummond than I do to you, after all.'

'Mary! Mary!'

'I say it again, I owe more to him than I do to you.'

'But he stole your child.'

'Yes, and you have made away with him. At least, you come and tell me that he is drowned. He went to sea by your orders. Is Barri drowned?'

'No, but he is an idiot.'

'He never was anything else,' said Mrs. Arnaud. 'I do not see why my son should be sacrificed, and Lady Rhyader's left in a mere state of idiocy. It is not just.'

'But you will not argue matters, Mary. You have lost your old sense. I cannot understand you. If I had been asked who was the most sensible woman in London, I should have named you. I am utterly surprised.'

'I will go to bed,' said Mrs. Arnaud, wearily. 'I cannot stand this any longer. I will go back to a religious life. I am not fit for the world.'

And so, she left Lord Festiniog without any further recognition.

CHAPTER VIII.

LORD FESTINIOG AND CLOTILDE.

Lord Festiniog and Mademoiselle Clotilde being left alone together, became at once confidential.

'You are an old friend, as I see, my lord,' she said. 'I have heard much of you.'

'Mademoiselle, if you will give me your confidence, I will value it like a mine of diamonds.'

'It is yours, with all my heart,' she said. 'She has not been a well used woman.'

'Certainly not,' said Lord Festiniog. 'My son Iltyd did not use her altogether well. For me, I behaved like a dog to her, once.'

'Your behaviour, my lord——' here she paused.

'Festiniog,' he suggested.

'I cannot pronounce *that*,' she said. 'I would if I could, but I can't. Say it again.'

He did so, and she made two or three attempts. They were no use, and she ended by saying that she, for the sake of argument, would call him M. Bonnechose. He agreed to this, and she continued.

'Your behaviour,' M. Bonnechose, was always very excellent to her. No one can find fault with you about it. She was married. Good. You did not know it. Good. You disputed it. That was right of you. Drummond had stolen her child. When that was proved and confessed to by Drummond, you allowed the fact. That was most honourable. But, were you good when you sent George Arnaud to sea with Barri? I do not think that you were.'

'But I did not know it. I did not know that the facts were proved.'

'Then I am misinformed,' said Mademoiselle Clotilde, 'that is all I can say.'

'Who was your informant?'

'Drummond,' she said.

'But, has he been making mischief between Mary and myself?'

'My lord, her position is this. He has told my cousin Arnaud, and she has told me, that since you have discovered the fact that George Arnaud is next in succession, you have been trying, in every way, to get rid of him. He will now say that you have succeeded in doing so; and, what is more, Marie might believe it.'

'But, is the man here, back in London, and saying such abominable falsehoods?'

'It is perfectly certain, and what is more, he has threatened your lordship in my presence.'

'The —— What does he threaten me with, then?'

'He only says that you are a lost man without him. He declares that your property is dependent on him, that you do not know where certain deeds are, and that you never dare to face him.'

'But when was he here last, yesterday?'

'No, this morning. He is in a very dangerous state. If I might detain your lordship, I would ask for a little advice. We want some, I assure you.'

'I will give you all that it is in my power to give,' said Lord Festiniog, 'but I must ask you again, what has Drummond been saying?'

'My lord, how can I say? He has been

telling Mrs. Arnaud that you are not Lord Festiniog at all, that there is some matter of an old marriage which he has discovered, that there is—I know not what. I cannot tell you, for I do not remember the whole.'

'What has Mary said to this?'

'She has been calm as usual. I think that she has been prepared for a journey.'

'Indeed.'

'Yes, but you must come back to-morrow. Do not delay here now.'

Lord Festiniog decidedly agreed that he would come back on the morrow.

CHAPTER IX.

THE CATASTROPHE.

Lord Festiniog went back to No. 17, and was extremely well-received there, by no one better than by old Madame Mantalent. Whatever that excellent old lady's temper might be previous to and after the arrival of Lord Festiniog, during his stay in the house, she was all sunshine.

A most pleasant chatty old woman; slightly and lightly scandalous at first, until she saw that Lord Festiniog did not like it; then, quite as scandalous as ever, but in a moral manner and without any levity. She pulled every body's character to pieces quite as charmingly as ever, but finding that Lord Festiniog was religious, she did it in a religious way, which was quite as poignant as the other way. She discoursed about the repentance, and ultimate (as far as she could tell) salvation of great sinners, with illustrative anecdotes, which became moral, from the tone of voice in which she told them. She let Lord Festiniog know, very soon, that she had repented, and then, treating him as a man on the verge of the grave, told him of what. His lordship told her that he was very glad to hear it, in fact, congratulated her. She received his congratulations with a smile, and hoped that he himself would some day find peace.

Madame always, during the short time which followed, treated Lord Festiniog as a repentant sinner, who might yet be saved. She never hinted at his turning Roman

Catholic, or at his marrying her last importation from France, Mademoiselle Clotilde. She always vilipended her spiritual director as a noodle, and ordered Clotilde out of the room when Lord Festiniog came. Still, to use a vulgarism, she took her change out of Lord Festiniog, by pointing out to him that he was the author of all the woes of her family. Had he been kinder to Iltyd, Iltyd never would have made a secret marriage; had he acknowledged Mary Arnaud's marriage at once, she never would have been thrown against James Drummond (which was totally untrue); had he, in short, done anything but what he had done, George Drummond never would have been drowned, Barri would not have been an idiot, and the last horrible catastrophe never would have occurred at all. Lord Festiniog was, in spite of his better reason, obliged to admit that it would have been better for him if No. 17 had never existed, and far better for No. 17 if he had never come near it.

The last disaster which had befallen this most unlucky number in that most unhappy street, is almost too terrible to be written down. Mary Arnaud had eloped almost openly, with James Drummond. They had started together from the London Bridge Station, they had been tracked to Paris, and so to Vienna, with all the acumen of an associated European police. At the last named town they were arrested, and discovered to be Lord and Lady Hartley on their wedding tour. A great deal of acrimonious correspondence followed, on the subject of this arrest, both at the time of which we are speaking and afterwards; still, the fact remained the same,

Mary Arnaud had gone off with James Drummond, and the ferocious virtue assumed by the injured family from Paris was an awful thorn in Lord Festiniog's side.

Why had they been pursued? Whose business was it to interfere with their arrangements? If Mary, who had lived so excellent and so virtuous a life, chose, at the end of it, to cast reputation to the winds, to go away with a man who had treated her in the most shameful manner, with the man who had actually stolen her child, now drowned, whose business was it, again? Why, no one's.

Drummond had played fast and loose with Lord Festiniog, but Lord Festiniog had forgiven him, and, on the whole, was kindly disposed to him. He was not the first man, thought Lord Festiniog, who went to the devil after a woman.

'As the late Mrs. Crawley said,' he added, for he was old, rich, and virtuous, 'I like the man's devotion to Mary, it is a fine trait in the man's character.'

'And Mary's devotion to Iltyd also,' thought his lordship, 'that is gone. A very good woman. I am sorry I ever quarrelled with her. Well, God forgive us all our sins. I'll go to No. 17 and talk to them all.'

So he went, and heard more particulars. It was only after a second visit there that he heard the whole truth from Rhyader, who met him at the shop door.

Mary Arnaud and James Drummond had not only gone off together, but had taken title and other deeds to the amount of two hundred thousand pounds with them. Hence, the hunt after them to Vienna—hence, the fact of the arrest of the innocent

Lord and Lady Hartley, who were twenty years younger than either of them. And hence the fact that Lord Festiniog, being persistently bullied by Lord and Lady Rhyader, was eternally at No. 17, very frequently, during the absences of Madame Mantalent, in the company of Mademoiselle Clotilde.

CHAPTER X.

AM RHEIN.

The dawn comes flushing up over the brown grey crags, and the shattered castles, lighting them one by one, and creeping lower and lower down the iron cliffs which confine the mighty river and hurl it in its anger from side to side of the glen. Wreaths of mist still linger among the closely packed vineyards, and along the dark rift of the Switzerthal, which on the opposite bank sends its flashing, sparkling contribution of water into the great Rhine itself. The swine herd's horn is heard, not unmusically, in the little town below, which is awaking to the tinkle of the bell for early mass. Now the sun reaches the river, and lights it with gleams of gold, green, and silver, most beautiful to behold; and now it has sketched out all the hills, and the solemn peace of the autumnal sabbath has settled down upon the beautiful Rhine lands.

Nowhere, neither on vineyard, on crag, on castle, on church tower, nor on wooded valley rich with the purple saffron, did the sun shine with more pleasant radiance than on the crucifix on the hill above the town, where the copse and vineyards end, and the broad cornfields clothe the level plateau as far as the eye can reach. Here four roads meet, and at the meeting place is the little shrine, with the great figure above it, a landmark for some miles either in sunshine or in snow.

Only one figure was in sight on this

morning, that of a woman kneeling in long devotion, with her head bent. So long did she remain in this attitude, that a little bird flew down and settled quite close to her, uttering a low, melancholy note. At length she rose, and turned her face towards the sunlight, looking round on the glorious prospect. It was Mary Arnaud.

Pale and harassed, but with a quiet, calm confidence in her face, which would have dispelled at once any fear of her, had it been seen by those most interested. The fresh morning air, and the pleasure of the landscape, put a slight colour in her cheeks as she set her feet down hill towards the town.

Some of the earliest risers in the place were the patients of Dr. Holland, who had, there, in the old convent of Marienburg, above the highest roofs, an establishment for people who were ill, or fancied themselves to be so. It was called a hydropathic sanatorium, but it was a very agreeable place, with quite as agreeable a table d'hôte as any near. The guests on this morning had returned from their early walks or baths, and had sat down to breakfast with the voracious appetite gained by foreign air and early hours, and there was a short silence, but very soon, conversation began and ran mainly on one point, the arrival of Mr. Hickson and his *distingué* looking sister the day before. They were discussed from every point of view, and it was agreed that she, at all events, would do. If they could get no other entertainment out of her, they could speculate about her and copy her exquisite clothes to the best of their ability.

On one side of the doctor sat the father

of the guests, a man of three seasons, a fat old gentleman from Porto Rico, and on the other the clergyman, a reverend London rector, a guest of two years. These two had the doctor's ear.

'And what shall you make of your new patient, doctor?' said Porto Rico.

'I am almost afraid I shall want your assistance,' said the doctor, turning to the reverend gentleman.

'Mind troubled?' said the reverend gentleman. 'Well, I have been used to sick beds for forty years, and I am ready for him.'

'I was not referring to spiritual consolation,' said the doctor, 'I meant that I fear I shall have to ask you to read the burial service over him.'

'So bad as that. Poor fellow! poor fellow! Ay! ay!'

'I fear so. He is in a state of intense nervous depression from which, if he does not rally ——' The doctor said no more.

'How fortunate that he has a relation with him,' said Porto Rico.

'She is most devoted to him,' said the doctor. 'I should be almost powerless without her. She has had him in this state or even worse, ever since Antwerp, and has only got him on by slow degrees. He would have died at Antwerp, were it not for her.'

'How did she manage to find us out, I wonder?' said the clergyman.

'I knew her in Paris,' said the doctor, 'I knew her family. And you two do me the favour not to talk about her at all; there are very painful family circumstances which render it as well not. Her brother has been living too hard, and also has met with some great disappointment. I can only say of her that she is the noblest of women.'

She entered shortly after he had finished speaking, and took her seat in the place which was left for her next the clergyman. She talked quite calmly about indifferent topics, the scenery, the air, the river, and then, turning to the doctor, asked him what he thought of her brother's state that morning.

'I think it is extremely grave, madam,' said the doctor. 'Still, such unremitting attention as yours must do more than I can. He is very uneasy without you.'

'I have been away from him this morning,' she said, 'for a lovely walk. I will spend the rest of the day with him.'

She went back to his room, and the doctor came with her. There, on a sofa before a window which looked down upon the Rhine, lay the miserable wreck called James Drummond, trembling at every sound, and staring at them as they entered with dilated pupils and quivering lips. He tried to speak, but he only produced an inarticulate babble. With the aid of the doctor's and Mary's arm he tried to walk across the room, but his knees smote together and they were afraid of his fainting. The doctor made a little weak brandy and water for him, but at the sight of it he gave an inarticulate howl, dreadful to hear, and fell back on his couch.

'He has been so ever since Antwerp,' said Mary. 'He cannot bear the smell of the brandy.'

'Yes, I will try opiates,' said the doctor. 'When did the worst of this begin, did you say?'

'At Antwerp, the day I joined him. In fact, I found him in the state I have mentioned to you.'

'He must have had some violent shock, surely, in addition to his intemperate habits.'

'Well, he had,' said Mrs. Arnaud. 'I was the cause of it.'

'H'm. Had you not better write home?'

'That is totally impossible,' said Mrs. Arnaud. 'Rhyader, or possibly Festiniog, would be thrusting their hands in and ruining everything. I must take the sole responsibility. Will he die?'

'I cannot say, it is very doubtful.'

'Will he speak before he dies?'

'He may or he may not. One thing is certain, for a long time no subject in the least degree likely to agitate him must be broached. That would be death.'

'Then I must wait here and watch.'

'There is no doubt of that if you wish to have him speak again reasonably. But reflect again, madame, is there not one friend to whom you could confide?'

'Not one, doctor. I have no friend whom I could trust—who would not commit an indiscretion. I could have confided in my poor drowned son, but he was lost in saving his cousin. No, I must go through it myself.'

So she took up her watch alone and unaided, and such a watch. Beside the couch of a man whom she had come to save, whose feeble hand, whenever it touched hers gave a gentle pressure which made her almost mad, whose eyes never met hers with an expression of tenderness and gratitude. Such was her watch, with the full sense that on his recovery, when she had wrested his secret from him, the poor wretch must be rudely undeceived as to her feelings for him, and by herself, by no other.

He had come to her wild with drink and rage, and had made a terrible scene. She had lost her temper, and had spoken words to him as fierce as any of his own, and so they had parted, as she believed, for the last time; it was not so, however; they were bound to meet again, and that suddenly.

Five hours after she had parted from him, she got a letter from him telling her that he was ruined, but that he was determined to drag down others in his ruin; that he was mad, but that he would make some others as mad as he was. He had taken Lord Festiniog's title deeds and securities to the value of two hundred thousand pounds, and was gone with them to America. One single word from her would stay him, even now, and it was to be sent by telegram to Gravesend, to a certain address.

She did not hesitate for an instant. She telegraphed the word 'yes,' and received in answer, 'Hotel du Parc, Antwerp. Hickson.'

She went to his office, and told his head clerk that she was going to join his master for a tour on the Continent, and that his letters were to be addressed to Vienna. The head clerk had long suspected that something of the kind would occur sooner or later between Mrs. Arnaud and James Drummond, and was not at all surprised. He no more believed they were going to Vienna, than he believed that they were going to Timbuctoo, but, like a good servant, he wished to cover his master's retreat, and did so, to the confusion of the police. A short note from Drummond, dated Gravesend, informed him that his master had not only gone abroad, but had taken Lord Festiniog's securities with him; at which point in the plot, he considered it necessary to communicate with Lord Rhyader, and save himself.

Meanwhile, Mary had found out that there was but one boat to Antwerp by which he could go, and taking a very hurried farewell of every one, she put herself on board of it. He joined the boat at Gravesend, and she kept close, watching him carefully, with her veil down.

He was very ill, so ill that it seemed to require an almost desperate effort on his part to get to his cabin. He had no servant, that was a comfort. His portmanteau was brought on board by the porters, and stowed with the other passengers' luggage. He went to his private cabin, at once, and lay down. They were hardly out of the Thames before Mary Arnaud took the Belgian captain into her confidence. She told him that her brother was very ill, and that she had followed him. As he was undoubtedly very ill, the captain pitied her, and gave her every assistance in his power when they got to Antwerp. At the Parc she had taken possession of him entirely, as his sister; but he was delirious and did not know her.

His keys, she had, but they revealed nothing. The papers were not in his trunks; that she very soon discovered. Where were they? No one knew, save the madman who lay gasping on the bed before her. The task before her was to save him until he could speak articulately and think consecutively. Then, she knew that she could have his secret from him, for she was certain on that one point.

But his disease fought terribly against nature, and it was only against overwhelming odds that she got him to St. Goar. There, to her horror, the thing which she longed for, yet dreaded, happened, the man began to recognise her, and to try and call her by name, to press her hand, and, as he in his vanity, thought, to believe that she had relented after all.

She watched him like a sister, no sister was ever more diligent or more faithful to a brother. And yet she hated the man. She had set a certain duty before her, that of recovering the lost papers for Lord Festiniog, 'who had been kind to her.' She knew, perfectly well, that if any of them interfered, the papers would be lost; and so, silent and unassisted, she kept watch over the man she liked least in all the world.

He began to mend before the beginning of October, and she began to dread the scene which must ultimately come. But that scene, which she had so often featured to herself, never came at all. Half the evils of this world are purely imaginary. The curse of successful nations like the Anglo-Saxon and Teutonic, is the anticipation of evil, as may be seen in our every day history, and is called familiarly, and somewhat foolishly, by the daily and weekly journals 'panic.' Mrs. Arnaud had prepared herself for a state of things which never occurred.

James Drummond got by degrees so much better, that he came to the table d'hôte, and ultimately went out driving with his reverence and Porto Rico. On his return from one of these drives, he asked Mary to come to his room, as he wished to speak to her very particularly.

She came, and sat down by him, not daring to begin the conversation.

'Mrs. Arnaud,' he said, 'they tell me that you have been utterly devoted to me during my illness. You must perceive that I am not long for this world, and I wish to make a clean breast as regards you, for my memory has quite come back now.'

'Yes, I have pulled you through, James,' she said.

'James! Ah, well, it is all the same now. If that word had been said like that years ago, things might have been different. For what reason, Mrs. Arnaud, have you paid this remarkable attention to me?

It was an awful question, an unanswerable question. Mrs. Arnaud sat dumb.

'I see that you cannot answer me. I thought for a while, during my delirium, that you had come after me for myself. Now that my intellect is restored, I know that you have only tended me to get the truth about Lord Festiniog's papers. So good a nurse should be properly repaid. You have ransacked my trunks, I suppose.'

Mary Arnaud was obliged to say, 'Yes.'

'Thank you. If you will open that one nearest the window you will find everything you want. No, not there my dear madam, nor there, neither, press that little spring on the lid; there you are.'

She stood up before him with the papers in her hand, but without a word to say for herself.

'Mary Arnaud,' he said, 'you are answerable for those papers, now, not I. Take them back to the people whom you always loved better than you did me. You are absolutely heartless.'

'Because I could not love you!' she flashed out.

'No, I am not a loveable person. But you are so utterly deceitful. You have saved my life for a few weeks, and you have tended me like a sister or a saint. And for what?—why, to get those papers. I have no gratitude towards you at all, you may take them and go to the devil with them.'

'May God forgive you, James Drummond, as I do,' she said, with the papers in her hand. 'Now, good-bye.'

'Stop, Mary,' he said, 'in decency's sake, stop; you must go through those papers, and give me a receipt for them: that is only fair.'

She was so silly and confused that she did it. She counted the papers, and gave a receipt for eight. The doctor and Porto Rico were called in to witness the document, which she left with him, and then she departed.

'Doctor,' she said to that functionary, 'I am going to England.'

'You cannot possibly take your brother, madam,' said he.

'I am aware of it; but I must go. Is his situation so critical?'

'I cannot tell at all. He may live to be eighty if he leaves off drinking *now*. I never thought that I should have pulled him through. I will take the best care of him.'

Mrs. Arnaud at once thanked him, and left the corridor with singular haste, the doctor thought. But the steamboat was nearly due, and she had to pack, a matter about which she was very nimble.

The steamboat did not come to the wharf,

the Rhine was low that year. She put off in a boat, with her trunks, and scrambled on board. James Drummond got from his bed and saw her go. He gave her *bon voyage.*

'Curse you, my lady,' he said. 'I have been angling at your worthless heels for too many years. You have tried to conceal your hatred from me, but you have not quite succeeded. You have been the cause of my drinking, a habit which never gave me any pleasure. I took to it because you scorned me, I leave it because you scorn me still. I think that I have prepared a nice little bed of nettles for you, madam, when you get home.'

The doctor came to see him later in the day. He was surprised to find his patient so much better. His patient entered into conversation with him.

'To what do you attribute my late illness, doctor?'

'To drinking.'

'Exactly. I have always hated it; and now I am going to give it up, for I never got any real pleasure from it.'

'It is time you did give it up,' said the doctor. 'You will not survive such another bout as this.'

'I know: it was that woman who has just gone, who drove me to it.'

'Your sister?'

'My sister! she is as much my sister as you are! She is one of the most swindling thieves in Europe. Has she paid her bill?'

The doctor thought it worth while to step down and inquire. Mary, certainly, in her haste, had not gone through that ceremony, and the doctor returned to inform him of the fact. The invalid laughed.

'You will find my cash-box in that trunk, doctor; bring it here and I will pay you.'

'My dear sir, there is no need to——' said the doctor.

'Bring it here, my dear sir, said Drummond. Short reckonings make long friendships.' The cash-box was brought to him, and the key of it was at the top of his dressing case. It was quickly opened.

The doctor saw on the top of a pile of bank-notes a yellow parchment, evidently very old. Drummond's trembling hand selected a note for 100*l.*, which he placed in the doctor's, begging him to carry on the account between them. The doctor received it gravely, and Drummond locked up the box with great rapidity. 'There is ten thousand or more here, doctor,' he said, 'but there are no thieves in Germany. I think that if you will send up Gretchen with some more of that draught, I will go to sleep.'

'Gretchen is in the kitchen,' said the doctor. 'If you do not mind new faces, I will send up the other woman; but, after all, I think that I had better bring you your sleeping draught myself.'

'It is all one to me,' said Drummond. The doctor gave it to him, and he went to sleep.

Drummond was fast asleep now, so fast asleep that he was nearly waking in eternity. Gretchen, the honest German woman, was really in the kitchen again, and had a hard day's work among the patients. The doctor met the 'new woman' on the stairs, and said to her, 'Carlina, you had better go up and sit beside Mr. Drummond.'

'Why do you call me Carlina?' she asked.

'It is your real name, is it not?' said the doctor, coolly. 'It is on your certificates.'

'Did the lady who has just left ever—?' said she.

'I should think it impossible,' said the doctor. 'I do not suppose that she would trouble herself much about you. I do not suppose that she has ever seen you.'

'I have taken good care about *that*,' said Carlina as she walked up stairs *to her duty*.

CHAPTER XI.

THE END OF JAMES DRUMMOND'S SCHEME.

Carlina approached James Drummond's bed with a curious mixture of feeling regarding him. She had loved the man, and, in one way, loved him still. He had used her as his plaything first, and afterwards as his tool. She had submitted to him, worked for him, and betrayed him to Lord Festiniog. She had done everything she could to ruin him, and bring him once more to her feet. She had not succeeded. Mrs. Arnaud always stood like a good angel between him and her. She had worked about through crafty, secret ways to separate them, but that seemed, last, impossible. When Mary Arnaud followed James Drummond, she followed also, and hid herself in the house where they had taken refuge.

She listened to what they said to one another on the occasion which has been described above. She saw that Mary Arnaud had never loved Drummond, and that Drummond had ceased to love Mary Arnaud.

'His heart shall be mine again,' she said. 'I will get a new power over him. Somehow, I care not how. I listened to every word which passed between them, and if you— (here she addressed her *daimon*)—mean to tell me that he told her the whole truth, I will be burnt alive.'

So she entered the sick man's room. He was sleeping very quietly; there was not the remotest need for her to hurry herself. She knew from spying where his keys were. She took out his cash-box and examined it. There were about six thousand pounds in notes. She first took two hundred-pound notes for necessary expenses, then she took three, then she took four, and locked up the cash-box, virtuously refusing to take another farthing. She came of a very decent banditti family, and the honour of her family appealed to her strongly not to take more than was absolutely necessary. She had actually locked up the cash-box, when the Neapolitan blood of her mother came through her head like a wave, and told her to take the whole seven thousand pounds. But then the blood of her father, who was a Genoese, and consequently a calculating man, a trader, came to her assistance, and said, 'The doctor knows that there is nearly ten thousand pounds here; if you take it all you will be found out.' She invoked the Virgin for this suggestion, which doubtless came from above. She opened the box, took out another hundred pounds, and felt transcendently virtuous.

Is she the only person in the world who has thought that she has made her peace with God by committing a small crime when she might have committed a greater one?

She went to look at the sleeping man. He was sleeping very quietly. She had been familiar with him in old times, and now she was but his nurse. He was lying, as she thought, uneasily, and she tucked his clothes in. A yellow old paper dropped from the tumbled clothes. She picked it up, and, taking it to the candle, read it through.

'You are one artful sinner, James Drummond,' she said. 'I see now why you got rid of that woman Arnaud in the way you did. After your illness you were tired of her. I can't think what you ever saw in her, myself. Now I have you in my hands, my lad. The doctor, when you unlocked the cash-box and gave it back could never have seen this; even *he* would not have withstood the temptation. Why, this paper is worth a hundred thousand pounds.'

Well, we will deal with this wondrous paper afterwards. It was worth nothing, but James Drummond and Lord Festiniog both thought that it was. Not to make any mystery, it was a grant of the whole Barri estates to Tom Killigrew, signed by Charles the Second. *There was no date*, and but one witness, whose name was undecipherable, but who had written pathetically under the word, 'Don't know what it is all about.'

She secured this paper, and then went to see after the sick man again. He was extremely quiet—so much so that she moved the bedclothes from his face. She looked at him only once—she had seen the thing before. She went down to the doctor at once and said, 'I wish you to come up with me.'

The doctor came, but fifty doctors could not alter circumstances—James Drummond was dead.

CHAPTER XII.

LORD FESTINIOG'S CONFESSION.

THE present writer is not the only person who considers that the practice of confession, as carried out in certain Communions, is a most objectionable thing. Still there is much to be said for it by its admirers. It is used in almost all sects under various names. Some call it 'confession,' some 'religious advice,' some 'experiences of conversion.' All mean, *to a certain extent only*, the same thing—the desire to confide to some one else what is too great a burden for your own heart. Lord Festiniog was one of the last men to go to confession, and yet he did so most decidedly.

It comes to very much the same thing in the end. People want to tell the truth and get excused, even if they are not Catholics.

Lord Festiniog wanted confession and absolution most emphatically. He knew that he could find some one to whom he could pour out his whole soul, and he knew that he could get excused, but he wanted to be absolved, and that his conscience told him that he could not very easily be.

There must be something very delightful in belonging to a religion which provides a not peculiarly literate man to answer for your sins. Lord Festiniog knew that no such easy-going faith was available in this world, but he got all that he wanted from a priest of the *Anglican* Church—that is to say, confession and absolution.

It occurred to him that as he was extremely vexed and worried in every way he would go and walk in Pall Mall. Why he should have done so is no business of ours. Pall Mall is not a place for a disturbed spirit. Lord Festiniog belonged to the Reform Club, but he was so vexed that he walked into the Travellers' by mistake, went into the morning room, and took up a newspaper.

The porter had followed him.

'Are you a member, sir?' that functionary asked. 'I do not know you.'

Lord Festiniog was going to swear, but a soft voice at his elbow stopped him.

'You have come here to see me, Lord Festiniog, I think?'

'If you choose to put it so,' said Lord Festiniog. 'Why—good gracious, it is Archdeacon Luxmore!'

'Let us come to the Athenæum,' said the archdeacon; 'we are both members there.'

And at the Athenæum Lord Festiniog made his confession to the archdeacon. We are about to betray the secrets of the confessional.

When they were settled comfortably Lord Festiniog said, 'You know, my dear archdeacon, that I am a fool?'

'My religion and my training as a gentleman prevent my ever contradicting anyone,' said the archdeacon.

'Exactly. If you like I will prove it to you,' said Lord Festiniog.

'I will take your word for fact, my dear friend,' said the Archdeacon. 'I am inclined entirely to agree with you without any proof.'

Lord Festiniog continued in a tone

which was at first cross, but which afterwards grew more genial and confidential:

'I never had much education in the ways of the world. I spoilt my two boys, and let them do pretty much as they liked. Gervase always did as I wished him, though I have had words with *him* at times. Iltyd never cared very much about me, but I loved him the best of the two. Do you understand me?'

'Perfectly.'

'Well, Iltyd took his own way when he grew up. He married a milliner. Mary is a most remarkable woman, archdeacon. Few women like her. I thought that she was not really married, and that Iltyd had deceived her. I and my son Rhyader treated her like one of the family, and she was our humble servant. After twenty odd years, she flew out at us, defied us, and said, and, what is more, proved that she was properly married at Leghorn.

'Good. We had a quarrel, but she won. And then comes the most remarkable part of the story. My lawyer, James Drummond, had access to her for business purposes in Italy, and fell in love with her; not in an ordinary way, but in a *mad* way. I will make matters as short for you as I can, but I must tell you that he was persistently *mad* about that woman, and that he stole her child, my own grandson, thinking by this means to engage her heart.'

'A curious way of doing it, was it not?' said the archdeacon.

'He thought,' said Lord Festiniog, 'that if she was left without any tie she would be more easily won. He adopted the boy he had stolen and brought him up. Now, the most astounding thing is this, archdeacon. Whether the man Drummond managed it or not I can't tell. After above twenty years of friendliness that woman, Mary Arnaud, quarrelled with me. She started as a milliner at No. 17, Hartley Street, and the very first person she met in her house *was her own son*, whom she did not know from Adam.'

'How on earth did that happen?' said the archdeacon.

'I don't know,' said Lord Festiniog, 'but happen it did. I did not know that the young man was my grandson. How should I? I liked him well enough, and of course would have done anything for him. In the meantime I drowned him.'

'That seems a mistake as it stands,' said the archdeacon.

'I did not mean to do it,' said Lord

Festiniog. I sent him abroad with Rhyader's son, as his tutor. He found out that he, in case of Barri's death, would be heir, and he—well——'

'Pitched the boy overboard?' said the archdeacon.

'Why, no; he drowned himself to save his rival.'

'A noble creature,' said the archdeacon. 'Well?'

'It is all very good to say "Well!"' said Lord Festiniog, testily. But everything is in the most infernal mess. Iltyd's son, who was called George Drummond, is drowned. The boy Barri seems a hopeless idiot in consequence of the sufferings he went through in his shipwreck. Mary Arnaud, Iltyd's own wife, after twenty-five years of good behaviour, has bolted to the Continent with my family lawyer, taking papers to the value of

100,000*l.*; taking, in fact, one which could not be replaced, and which would utterly ruin me if it was discovered.'

'What could that be?' said the archdeacon, for priests are curious.

'Well, my dear sir, if that paper was correct, I am no more Lord Festiniog than you are the Pope of Rome. This is safe with you?'

'Certainly; I am accessory after the fact,' said the Archdeacon. 'Proceed in the tale of your wrongs.'

'I think that I ought to be treated with more respect by Rhyader and I have fallen in love. At seventy—what do you think of that? What advice do you give me?'

'You seem to have made a tolerable mess of it among you,' said the archdeacon. 'If I was in your place I should most certainly do nothing. What is the missing paper, and who is your new lady-love?'

'Well, never mind about the lady; I may get over that business; I have done so once or twice before. The paper is a grant of all we hold to the Killigrews by Charles the Second.'

'That,' said the archdeacon, 'is dangerous; and you should not have told me. However, I will shrive you on condition that you do the right.'

And what was that?

CHAPTER XIII.

A SURPRISE FROM MADAME MANTALENT.

Lord Festiniog had long ago decided that life would be worth having were it not for its troubles. At nearly the same time Cornewall Lewis had come to the conclusion that life would be possible without its pleasures. Victor Hugo would make out that they both meant the same thing. But we are not so clever as Victor Hugo, and are perfectly certain that they meant something entirely different. Lord Festiniog desired quiet, diligent action, and Sir George Lewis did not. Lord Festiniog said always that the women were driving him to the deuce in his old age. Sir George Lewis never said anything of the kind.

Lord Festiniog, however, had very hard times. He was sitting one evening with Mademoiselle Clotilde at No. 17, when the door was opened, and the renegade Mary Arnaud walked in, and, without the least remark, took off her bonnet, placed it on the sofa, and requested Lord Festiniog to poke the fire; she then sat down.

'I want some tea,' she said to Clotilde; 'I have been travelling.'

Clotilde departed with amazing alacrity, and left Mary and Lord Festiniog alone together, to his immense horror. He felt that an explanation must come, and he hated explanations.

'Well, my lord,' she began, 'I think that

I have made everything right for you. Here are the papers.'

'The papers which you took, Mary?'

'The papers which I took? I think you mean the papers which he took. I got them from him. Here they are.'

'I thought that you had been false to me,' said Lord Festiniog.

'Then you must be a noodle,' said Mary Arnaud. 'Look at these papers. They are, I fancy, correct. After trusting me so many years, you might trust me for a few more.'

Lord Festiniog looked at her with admiration, and then he went through the papers. 'Mary,' he said, 'you only went with the poor fellow who is dead, to get these papers for us?'

'I do not understand you, my lord. I went with him to get these papers. I allow that. That I was true to Iltyd—I neither insult myself nor you by going further with the matter. I got these papers from him; but you speak of him as dead: I left him mending.'

'I have had a telegram which tells me that he is dead, however.'

And Lord Festiniog watched her carefully to see how she would take the news.

'Poor James,' said Mary Arnaud without a show of emotion: 'and so he is dead. Poor fellow. He loved me very tenderly, and I liked him, to some extent. But I am not sorry that he is dead, on the whole.'

'My dear Mary—'

'Your dear Mary! Has not the man been the very bane of my whole life? A falser friend never existed, neither to you nor to me. Can I possibly pretend to a regret which I do not feel? Are you sorry?'

'You are so terribly blunt,' said Lord Festiniog. 'I don't mean to say that I am very sorry.'

'Then, what do you suppose I am,' said Mrs. Arnaud, 'at the removal of the irritation of my life? Lord Festiniog, do you know that when I left him he hated me?'

'Perhaps,' thought the old man, 'that may have something to do with your singular coolness about him.' And he quietly went over the abstracted papers.

'The only paper which was of any vast value,' said he, quietly, 'is not here; your errand has been perfectly fruitless, I am sorry to say. He lied roundly, and has utterly deceived you. The paper which would ruin us is missing.'

'I thought that he was rather easy with me,' said Mrs. Arnaud. 'What is to be done now, in the name of goodness? Has he destroyed it, do you think, in spite?'

'I wish to heaven he had,' said Lord Festiniog. 'I was a fool to keep it so long, I know that. If Rhyader knew of it! But he cannot have destroyed it; it would be a most friendly action.'

'Well, I don't know what is to be done *now*,' said Mrs. Arnaud. 'He knew the contents of this paper, of course.'

'Why, of course he did, my dear soul, he *found* it, and pointed out its value to me. Don't you know that he said to you once that I was not Lord Festiniog at all? If another family gets hold of that paper I am poorer than the poorest beggar who whines for pence at a crossing. If it is known that I had it in my possession, and was ever aware of its contents, I should be utterly disgraced as well as ruined. In God's name keep all this from Rhyader—don't let a soul alive know of what has passed between us.'

'How charmingly you look to-night, dear Lord Festiniog,' said a voice, which made them both start to their feet, with an exclamation of terror from the lady, and a loud oath from the gentleman.

There, behind them, stood old Madame Mantalent, charmingly dressed and smiling; they were absolutely dumb with utter horror.

'I have been listening to you two for the last five minutes,' she said, 'and have heard every word you uttered. I am a most unscrupulous listener; I learnt the habit at my *magazin* in Paris, where, to tell the truth, I made money by it. The instant I heard Marie's voice in the passage, I pulled my old rheumatic bones upstairs, and here

I am. You, Lord Festiniog, look as though you wished that I was anywhere else.'

'Madam, I have not that power of concealing my thoughts, which is possessed in such an eminent degree by your charming nation, and by no member of it more than yourself. I wish, madam, you had been at— (he was going to say Jericho, but substituted)—Paris before you had heard what you have.'

'My lord,' said the old woman, with a strange indescribable radiance in her face, which utterly puzzled and surprised Lord Festiniog; 'my lord, try to recall what I *have* heard.'

'You have heard me confess my own dishonour, madam.'

'Ay!' cried the old woman, 'and I have heard my daughter vindicate *hers*, and so, what is yours to me? My own long-suffering

Marie, take your mother's blessing, and try to forgive her for ever distrusting you.'

They were between the door and him, and so Lord Festiniog was obliged to escape to the window, against which he leant while there was silence in the room, broken only by a few sobs.

CHAPTER XIV.

LORD FESTINIOG'S COURTSHIP.

'Now, my dear people,' said Madame Mantalent, sinking quietly on the sofa, 'we three had better put our heads together over this business. This paper must be got hold of and burnt. I have managed a few things in my time, and I fancy that you could not have a better adviser.'

'Madam, certainly not!' said Lord Festiniog, 'but you must perceive, from what I have let fall, that my honour is in your hands. I can move no further in the matter. My hands are clean about it (which was a fiction). I cannot tell what I shall do.'

'There is one thing you will not do,' said Madame Mantalent; 'you will not act, or speak to Lord Rhyader, or any other human being, until you have consulted with us. You will promise that?'

Lord Festiniog thought for a little; at last he said:—'Yes, I will promise that, I think that I can say that much.'

'To be sure,' said Madame Mantalent; 'and come to us to-morrow morning. We will do nothing until we see you, you may depend upon that.'

So Lord Festiniog went.

He knew that he was partly consenting to a dishonourable action. He most entirely thought that his son Rhyader would have gone at once to the other family, and told the whole truth to their utter ruin. Yet he could not determine what to do. As he went downstairs, there was nothing, as it appeared to him, staring him in the face but utter, sheer ruin. He was not like a man beside himself, because old training had given him the habit of keeping his thoughts to himself, but he was utterly and entirely at his wits' end.

As he came into the hall, Clotilde came to meet him with a light.

'My lord,' she said, 'come into the little back parlour, which is now empty, and speak to me; I see from your face that you are in great trouble, you must let me share it.'

He followed her in, and sat beside her on the sofa.

He came very near her, but she did not seem to object in any way whatever. He took her hand in his, and she did not withdraw it; and then he made a fool of himself, not for the first time in his life.

'Clotilde,' he said, 'I am a very old man, is it in any way possible that you can love me? I will try to make you— '

'You need not try,' said Clotilde. 'I do love you beyond any other man in the world.'

'But, Clotilde. some terrible things have happened. I dare not ask you for your hand until—until—I know not when.'

'For my hand!' said Clotilde, wondering, 'you have got it, have you not—at least my right hand? You shall have the other, if you like.'

'I mean your hand in marriage.'

She stared at him, but without withdrawing her hand. 'Why, you never thought of marrying *me*?'

'I certainly did.'

'My dear lord, pray banish the idea at once and for ever. I like you better than any man I have ever seen, except my grandfather, who was very like you, though I fancy he had more of the grand air than even you have. Come, there is a kiss for you, grandpapa. If I ever marry anyone, I will ask you to give me away. But I fancy, myself, I do not care about a husband, husbands and wives perpetually disconcert one another; there is only one other man in the world who can make himself a worse nuisance to a woman than her husband.'

'Who is that?' said Lord Festiniog, 'her brother?'

'Oh, no! her lover,' replied Clotilde. 'Brothers are by no means objectionable. If you quarrel with them you can make it up again; and, even if you do not, they never shoot themselves, or another man, or, what is still more important, yourself. Husbands and lovers are a mistake. Now, we will be real friends.'

'Certainly,' said Lord Festiniog, and before he had time to say more, she went on—

'Look at Darcy and Heloise, I would not change places with her, although she has become Lady Hartop. Nobody cares to receive her, because she kept shop here. No, every one is not so generous as you are, Lord Festiniog; we will be friends, if you please, but nothing else.'

'Well! well!' said Lord Festiniog, 'I would have made you happy, in my way. Be happy in your own.'

'My dear grandpapa,' said Clotilde, 'will you have the goodness to consider what a life we should have led with the Rhyaders if we had ever married?'

'Hah!' said Lord Festiniog. 'Well, my dear—yes—I did not think of that. It is better as it is; oh, yes! it is far better as it is, though he did urge me once.'

'Now, then, we are comfortable,' said Clotilde. 'Tell me now, as we are in entire confidence, what is going on upstairs?'

'But I promised not to mention the matter to any human being if I recollect.'

'If you don't tell me all about it, I will tell Rhyader that you proposed to me,' said Clotilde.

Lord Festiniog forgot, at once, his duties as senator, father, and gentleman. He told Clotilde every word of what had passed upstairs, but bound her to secresy as regarded every other human being in the whole world.

'I shan't tell anybody,' she said. 'I wish it had been possible to tell Heloise, for she is the most artful little minx in the world; but she has made the mistake of marrying, and is therefore unworthy of confidence. She would tell her husband. You had better leave the matter with those two souls upstairs.'

'I suppose I had better for the present, but I am sorely puzzled, and I dare not tell Rhyader. You have been a kind friend to me, Clotilde—'

'And have prevented you making a fool of yourself,' she added.'

'Hardly yet,' said Lord Festiniog, 'that still depends on the powers above,' and he pointed accidentally with one of Clotilde's fingers, and not his own, to the upper story, where Madame Mantalent and Mrs. Arnaud were seated in conclave.

At this moment there came a loud knock at the door. They drew suddenly apart and were silent.

This last incident may appear strained

and improbable to those critics who do not reflect that the same thing happens in most London houses at least once in five minutes, and that they had been talking for at least twenty *without* its happening. The improbability of the thing lies in its not having happened before.

Some people were in the passage asking for Lord Festiniog. 'By heaven,' that nobleman exclaimed, 'they are coming in here.' And, indeed, Rachel opened the door, and admitted Mrs. Arnaud's colly dog, before heard of in these pages. Clotilde, with the fervour of her nation, at once caught him to her bosom and carried him to the opposite sofa. But that did not prevent Rachel announcing Lord Rhyader and Mr. Barri; nor did it prevent Lord Festiniog from sitting bolt upright with an expression on his face like that of a man who has robbed a bank, and is fully conscious of having the whole proceeds on his person when he is arrested by the police.

Suppose that terrible old Mantalent was to hobble into the room now, and make some frightful disclosure before she could be stopped. Suppose she ever were to know the frightful nonsense which he had been talking to Clotilde. Suppose—well, he supposed everything which a guilty man will when he fears detection, and he looked such a perfect noodle that his own son scarcely recognized him.

'How are you, father?' said Lord Rhyader.

'I don't know,' said Lord Festiniog. 'I thought I did this morning, but I'll be hanged if I do now.'

The boy came towards him, but very unsteadily. Lord Festiniog met him and put him on the sofa beside him. 'This is one of your bad days, Barri, eh?'

'Yes,' said Barri, 'one of the days when everything goes round. But I am getting very much better, grandpa. I am beginning to read a little again now. You will never make a man of me, but you may make a scholar. Poor George Drummond, he died to save me, though it was against his interest. My heart would break with joy if I saw him again.'

'We will not,' said Lord Rhyader, 'pursue that subject. George Drummond is drowned. Barri, go upstairs and see Madame Mantalent: who, the servant tells me, is there.'

'No!' said Lord Festiniog, sharply, 'send the boy into the street to walk about. Mademoiselle Heloise, would you mind leaving us, and taking the dog with you?'

He went, and he opened the door for her, kissed her hand. He then sat down, looking anything but a noodle now, and confronted his son.'

'Are you going to marry *that* lady, sir?' said Rhyader, haughtily, thereby putting the battle-field entirely in his father's hands.

'No, sir!' said Lord Festiniog. 'I asked her to marry me just now, and her answer was at once dignified and sensible. She pointed out the difference in our ages, and, what is more, she showed what extreme opposition I should meet with from you. I desired to marry that lady, sir, and I asked her. She has refused me.'

'She is a young lady of great sense,' said Lord Rhyader.

'That is a civil thing to say to your own father, sir,' said Lord Festiniog, who above all things wished to get into a passion, with some show of reason. 'I do not see that I have done anything to give you reason to insult me.'

'My dear father—'

'There, enough, sir, you can go. I desire to hold no more communication with you at the present moment. I am using every endeavour to keep a house over your head, and I am met in this way.'

'But I assure you, my dear Lord—'

'I am not,' said Lord Festiniog, now nearly laughing, but taking a lesson from the school of Mademoiselle Clotilde, 'to be pacified by endearments, however plausible. I request you to leave me, sir, and to believe that I am working for your good.'

'I cannot understand it,' said Lord Rhyader; 'why have you turned against me suddenly, after so many years?'

'Rhyader, go away. There is more

hatching in this old No. 17 than you dream of or must know about.

Lord Rhyader thought it best to go ; and as he led poor struggling Barri along he thought, very sadly, that his father was losing his head, and that he would soon be master of the family.

CHAPTER XV.

MADAME MANTALENT GOES ON THE WAR TRAIL.

'Mamma,' said Mrs. Arnaud, when they were alone together, 'did you actually suspect me?'

'My love, I did.'

'Then you must make amends.'

'Yes, in what way?'

'First, you must in future be kinder to all of us than you have hitherto been; and secondly, you must assist us by the whole power of your brain.'

'I promise both things, my darling. Now let us get to work at once and lose no time. From whom did Lord Festiniog get this telegram announcing James Drummond's death?'

'From Doctor Holland.'

'I suppose that the dead man must have told him to telegraph to his lordship, then. You know more about the late man than any one else: had he any relations?'

'None, that I am aware of.'

'What sort of a man is Dr. Holland? An upright man?'

'One of the noblest and most upright of men,' said Mrs. Arnaud.

'That is a terrible nuisance. It is the way of the world. You can find rogues enough when you don't want them, and then when you want one particular man to be a rogue, you find him an honest man.'

'Why do you desire him to be dishonest, mamma?'

'It is fortunate that your mother was born before you, simpleton,' said the old lady. 'Do not you see that by this time he has made an inventory of the dead man's goods, and has the paper in his possession?'

'That is perfectly true,' said Mrs. Arnaud.

'How long were you there with him, did you say?'

'About a fortnight.'

'What did you represent yourself to be?'

'His sister.'

'Cannot you go back in the same capacity, and take possession of everything? Why of course you can.'

'I am sorry to say that we are checkmated there again,' said Mrs. Arnaud.

'Why?'

'That woman Carlina, who helped him to take George from me at Ravenna, had followed him there, and she would be pretty sure to tell the truth, if it was only to spite me.'

'That does not follow,' said madame. 'Post away and try; you can do no harm by that. Go and see how the land lies.'

'It is rather a difficult thing for me, but if you advise —.'

'I'll tell you what,' said the old lady, 'I'll go with you.'

'My dear mamma, with your rheumatism!'

'I shall howl occasionally,' she said, coolly; 'you will explain the reason of that to our fellow-voyagers if they exhibit any symptoms of terror or alarm. All my pain will be amply compensated for if I can have the opportunity of matching my art against a woman. You are an excellent woman, but you are a nigaude, my dear. This Italian woman may be worth talking to. I daresay that she will give us a vast deal of difficulty, but all that will be intense pleasure to me. I only live in a world of excitement. Get the things ready, and we will start to-morrow morning.'

'But what are we going to do?' said Mrs. Arnaud. 'It seems fearfully like a conspiracy.'

'It *is* one, my dear,' said Madame Mantalent. 'But you must help in it. The family were very kind to you. And moreover, you can scarcely help yourself, because by representing yourself as the dead man's sister, and getting possession, with your usual cleverness, of every paper but the right one, you are deep in it already.'

This was obviously true, and Mrs. Arnaud abandoned herself to her fate, only remarking to her mother that they must be very careful, or that they would find themselves in Coldbath Fields prison.

Madame Mantalent assented to this. 'It shows you, my dear,' she said, 'how extremely careful we should be. Don't commit yourself and don't sign anything. Allow me to observe that it is not good *ton* to speak to a woman with chronic rheumatism (and that woman your own mother) of Coldbath Fields. It is sufficient of itself to bring on a violent lumbar attack.

'Well mamma, I trust you, and I will do everything you tell me. I have given you very much trouble in my life, and I will try to be dutiful now.'

'The result of which, my dear, will be that we shall probably end our days in jail. English jails are, I believe, very insufferable, but they cannot possibly be worse than the streets of London. In jail, my dear, there are neither shoeblacks, costermongers, nor whistling boys. If they place a shoeblack outside my cell, I have about me, in my stockings, the means of putting an end to an existence which Providence evidently had decided to have lasted too long.'

'But you don't carry poison in your stockings, mamma,' said Mrs. Arnaud, anxiously.

'Far from it, my dear. I only speak as a milliner. From my knowledge of textile fabrics I could hang myself in my stockings most dexterously, that is all.'

'I could easily cut you down, mamma,' said Mrs. Arnaud, anxious to keep the old lady in good humour

'My dear, no,' she replied. 'I get my stockings from a French firm, not from an English one. Go down and see if Lord Festiniog has gone.'

The report was that Lord Festiniog had been gone a long time. That Lord Rhyader had been there with Barri. That Clotilde was waiting supper, and that everything was quiet. Madame Mantalent descended to the little back parlour in better humour than she had been in for some years.

The aged female warrior scented a battle. The quarrel was none of hers, but the fighting was by no means less pleasant for that. In the middle ages Italians, Germans, Poles, Swiss, nay even it is said English, Scotch, and Irish, used to take part in wars with which they had logically no connection whatever. Mr. Dugald Dalgetty had no personal quarrel with any human being, and had very few political ideas. Madame Mantalent wished well to her species, but she liked fighting them. She was hungering for a battle when she came down to supper. She had made a grand *pax* with Mrs. Arnaud, which she intended to keep—in the first place because she really admired her; in the second place because she had got to love her; and in the third place because she was dead afraid of her. She argued that from her late conduct you could never tell what Mary Arnaud would do next; she was like a fire or torpedo ship, and Madame Mantalent wished to be in command.

At the same time it was not to be supposed that the old lady had got rid of her temper all at once; she wanted an object for it, and she discovered one in Clotilde. When she had eaten her supper she ordered off Mrs. Arnaud to pack up, and then asked Clotilde, in the presence of Rachel, who was clearing away,

'Are you going to marry Lord Festiniog?'

'No.'

'Has he asked you?'

'Yes.'

'You are a fool, if ever there was one in this world. All my family appear to be idiots.'

Mrs. Arnaud suddenly appeared in the doorway. 'Mother,' she said, 'what did you promise?'

'Right, child,' said the old lady. 'Clotilde. I am sorry for what I said. Rachel, there is the baker ringing at the door-bell. Clotilde, put me to bed, for I cannot disguise from you, my dear, that Marie and I are bound for a long journey to-morrow.'

Clotilde took her aunt to bed, helped to undress her, and tucked her in. This took a considerable time, because, although the old lady was by no means 'made up,' yet—well—she had the habit of making a long toilet, both when she went to bed and when she got out of it.

On this occasion her toilet was assisted by a character which has scarcely appeared in these pages: Mrs. Arnaud's colly dog, the one which was sent to her from the religious house in which she had lived so long. Rover got on the old lady's bed when she was putting that finishing touch to her hair which some old ladies consider necessary before they go to sleep, lest, we suppose, death should overtake them before they awake, and hurl them into eternity with their hair out of curl. Rover, we say, got on the bed and licked her face. The old woman did not hit him with her hair-brush, but spoke kindly to him. She noticed that Rachel was in the room, and asked her to put her pillow straight: this from her was a compliment.

'A long journey to-morrow, Rachel,' she said; 'and then the long journey of all. You will try to remember me kindly, Rachel, will you not?'

Rachel was about to reply, when Mrs. Arnaud entered suddenly. She was very pale, and her eyes were a little dilated, but she was perfectly firm.

'Clotilde and Rachel, go upstairs. By this door. Leave the dog.'

They went, and she sat on her mother's bed. The dog growled, but she laid her hand on his neck and he was pacified.

'Mother! mother!' she said. 'What shall we do now? There is a message from the sea.'

'I always believed that there would be,' said the old woman, rising in her bed. 'I have dreamt of it, and prayed for it. Where is he?'

'Will you let the man come in and speak for himself?'

'What, George?'

'No, only a sailor.'

'Let him come at once,' said the old lady. A Frenchwoman who knows how to manage her complexion is afraid of no man.'

CHAPTER XVI.

WHAT MADAME MANTALENT DID WITH HER WATCH.

Few contrasts ever seen in this world could ever have been greater than that between the old Frenchwoman sitting up in her bed, and the sailor who came into the room. Her complexion was like a very pale rose—his was very much like a rather badly burnt brick. But they had something in common: they both had grand bold black eyes; and Mrs. Arnaud, standing in an atmosphere composed of eau de cologne on the side of her mother, and bad tobacco on the side of the sailor, came to the conclusion that neither of them were particularly afraid of anything.

'Madam,' said the sailor, 'I hope I see you well.'

'I am rheumatic, sir,' she said; 'but otherwise perfectly well. I am bound for a journey to-morrow. Will you state your intelligence?'

'I come to speak of Mr. George Drummond, madam,' said the sailor. 'He requested me to come, in case I should escape. He said that his relations lived here, and I have done as he told me.'

'You see, sir,' said Madame Mantalent, 'his grandmother and his mother, pray proceed.'

'When the "Newcastle" was lost, madam, I stayed with him and with the captain. When she went down—we all three on the same piece of wreck—and a very few hours passed before we were seen by two ships. They both bore down upon us at once. One apparently homeward bound, got nearer to us quicker than the other, but passed a little to leeward. I left the spar and struck out for her, because I wanted as a poor man to get home. The captain and Mr. Drummond not being such active swimmers as I am, preferred to risk being taken up by the other ship, and I saw them both taken on her deck, apparently safe and sound. I expected to have been home long ago, but, with my usual luck, the Italian bark which picked me up lost her foremast and was driven out into the Atlantic by the easterly wind which followed the gale. We were glad to make the west coast of France before we were right. Here I got a berth back to the Mediterranean, and telegraphed to my wife from Brest. The French people made such a mess of my

English that she never understood any more than that I was alive, and as our owners had paid her as if I was dead, she didn't bother them. But, to make a long story short, both the captain and Mr. Drummond were taken safe on board an outward bound ship.'

'But did she not signal her name?' said sharp Madame Mantalent.

'She did, madam, but I fairly tell you that if she had I should not have remembered it. I was very much knocked about by the sea. I can only repeat that Mr. Drummond was perfectly safe when I saw him last.'

'On board the outward bound ship?' said Madame Mantalent.

'By no means, madam. I have seen Mr. Drummond since. I have seen him at Bordeaux. He is coming to England as fast as he can, but his leg was broken, it seems, and for some reason or another he seems in no hurry.'

'There is no great reason for him to hurry,' said Madame Mantalent. 'Well, sir, we are very much obliged to you. Would you kindly accept my watch? It is a Brequet, and of no use to you, I dare say, but you can exchange it for an English chronometer, you know. So, good bye.'

'Stop one moment, sir,' said Mrs. Arnaud, speaking to the sailor, with Madame's watch in his hand.

'Did Mr. Drummond tell you by what route he was coming home? I am his mother, and I wish to see him.'

'I can tell you that, madam, I think,' said the sailor. 'He was coming through the Alps, and down the Rhine.' And so the sailor departed.

'What are we to do now, mother?' said

Mrs. Arnaud. 'Is there any use for my trying to intercept him?'

'Not the remotest, my dear. He would be of no earthly use in any way whatever. You and I have to commit what the world would call a crime together; and, to tell you the truth, I would rather that your son was out of the way, at this moment. He is alive, and that is enough for you. Let him go. You and I must hunt in couples, and get that paper back. I think we owe that to the family. We will start to-morrow morning.'

The intelligence of the declaration of a most bloody war, or the result of a University boat race, generally arrives at some parts of Her Majesty's dominions long before the fact has scientifically taken place. The telegraph has set back the dial of Ahaz. Science triumphs when she tells us that things are known in Constantinople before they have (chronologically) happened in England. The sun is too slow for us. The University race is, according to Calcutta time, rowed at midnight, and they get the result of it on their breakfast tables, in the early morning, just when our children are being put to bed.

Mrs. Arnaud and Madame Mantalent started early in the morning to catch Carlina and bargain with her about the lost paper. Neither of them had travelled very much, and they thought that they were making good speed.

CHAPTER XVII.

MADAME MANTALENT DEFEATS ENGLAND AND PRUSSIA.

In due course of time they arrived at St. Goar. Madame had behaved very well, and was singularly gracious. She occasionally showed slight symptoms of rheumatism by giving wild yells in improper places, but she was very amiable. At Aix-la-Chapelle she howled in the middle of high mass, and being asperged with holy water by a priest on her back, for the purpose, as he afterwards explained, of driving the evil spirit out of her, shook her fist in secret, and said words about the Roman hierarchy which we decline to repeat, both on religious and on political grounds. Ultramontane as madame most emphatically was, she uttered words which are more fitly left, in our opinion, to the ear of her spiritual director than to that of our readers. She simply expressed her opinion about the too liberal use of holy water in a way which might have satisfied the gentleman who is traditionally supposed to have an extreme horror of it in any form. The fact is, that she referred the ministering priest personally *to* that gentleman. It was a mistake on her part, clearly; but we only say that Madame Mantalent behaved, for her, like an angel.

Mary Arnaud was always good-natured. She was a trifle colourless, perhaps, but she was always resolute enough and good-natured enough. She had a way of viewing life which was a little different to that of ordinary people. Nothing would ever have induced her to commit a crime for herself, but she did not hesitate to do anything very strange indeed for those she loved, and who had been kind to her. Of course she ought to have been a heroine, and have refused to act in the matter of this paper; but alas! she was no more of a heroine than old Madame Mantalent, who would, now her blood was up, have most willingly injured Carlina and half a dozen more people who stood in her way.

You are angry with Lord Festiniog. He behaved shamefully, there is no doubt about that. His duty was perfectly clear. 'He should never have concealed that paper, in which he believed. He should have done his duty. He should have put it in the hands of the family, and have gone out into the world a beggar; leaving Rhyader, his wife, Barri, and George Drummond without one solitary penny in the world. But he was a very immoral old man, and he did not see his way to doing it.

It may be supposed that, with an honest old gentleman like Lord Festiniog, there was some mental struggle about the matter. That he thought he was doing wrong, is perfectly certain, but there was no mental struggle whatever. He was called upon, as he thought, to give up so many thousands a year, which his family had enjoyed, not entirely without benefit to the State, for two centuries. He determined most emphatically not to do it, and he invoked a malediction on his own head, similar, though rather stronger than that used by Madame Mantalent in the Dom Kirk of Aachen, if he did anything of the kind.

His idea was that the deed would be

brought to him, and that he could buy it. He had a faith about that, because the deed was worth more to him than to anyone else. He let the two women go to see what they could discover, and with a degree of cowardice, stopped at home himself, to see what they could do.

The women were avenged on him; they had considerably better times than he had. Had that excellent old lady, Madame Mantalent, known, while she was travelling up the Rhine, with her daughter, what a tremendous pickle Lord Festiniog was in at No. 17, I am afraid that her amiability would have become angelic. It was one of the great points in that sainted woman's character that she was always most cheerful when she saw her fellow-creatures in distress. She would have *loved* Lord Festiniog, had she known the state of affairs at No. 17.

She would have given him money. She would have lent him her air-cushion. She would have sat by his bedside till he swore at her, and then have sat like a saint. Alas! she never saw Lord Festiniog in his agony. She would have given all she was worth for it, but it was denied her.

They arrived at St. Goar. Mrs. Arnaud took rooms, and then went to see the doctor. He was in his room, and she knocked at the door; they interchanged greetings, but Mrs. Arnaud saw at once that the doctor was cool.

There was a little indifferent conversation about the death of James Drummond, and then she said:—

'I have come mainly about my poor brother's papers and effects.'

'Mrs. Arnaud,' he said, 'I am very sorry to say that I cannot put myself in communication with you on the subject. Before I give up one single paper, you must swear before the Mayor that you are his sister.'

'I can't do that,' said Mrs. Arnaud, promptly. 'I would if I could, but I cannot. I am not his sister. Now you have the whole truth.'

'Good!' said the doctor. 'Are you any relation to him?'

'No. May I look through his things?'

The doctor hesitated, and then said:—

'Mrs. Arnaud, you inspire such confidence, that I will do wrong and say yes.'

'God bless you for that,' said Mary Arnaud. 'Come, I will tell you this much of the truth. The man loved me, but I could never love him. He did me the most irreparable wrong that man could do to woman, yet I was kind to him at last.'

'Most kind. He did not marry you?'

'Sir,' she said, 'you utterly mistake me.

He did me a wrong, inconceivably greater than the one of which you are thinking. He got me away alone after Iltyd's death, and he stole my child, with the assistance of that woman, Carlina, who is here now. It was done at Ravenna, and that woman knows it. I forgave him because he, for my sake, brought the boy up as his own son; and the boy is alive, and, I hope, will live to comfort my old age.'

'Will you, Mrs. Arnaud,' said the doctor, 'kindly tell me what you wish me to do? Yours is a very singular story, and I have the very firmest faith in it. But, my dear madam, the last time you left here, you carried away a large number of his papers; and I would greatly prefer the presence of a notary before you go through his effects.'

'My dear doctor, you are stronger than I am, and I am not likely to *steal* any of his papers. Let us, by all means, have a notary, and I will go through them with you.'

'I shall be most happy to do so,' said the doctor, 'but you spoke just now of the woman Carlina. She has left this place.'

'Yes?'

'Yes; she has gone, I believe, to England, but I am not sure. However, if you will wait I will send for the notary, and do as you desire.'

'May my mother be present, doctor?'

'Surely, Mrs. Arnaud, I will agree to that.'

The notary came, the effects were examined, but the paper was not to be discovered.

The poor man had brought away at least seven thousand pounds with him, that was found perfectly secure; but there was no trace whatever of the important document. The notary got a little impatient.

'Mrs. Arnaud,' he said, in perfectly good English, 'you, under pretence of being the dead man's sister, carried off to England his papers. That is a matter which you cannot deny.'

This was turning the tables with a vengeance.

'I took away the papers which he gave me,' said Mary Arnaud.

'My dear madam, that is no answer.'

'I don't know anything about answers,' said Mrs. Arnaud. 'I wish I had never come here.'

'That is likely, madam. You confess to having carried off his papers under false pretences. I am afraid I must ask the Mayor to put you under arrest. It seems rather a black case. It was a terribly black case,' the notary continued; 'in the Continental fashion of believing everyone to be guilty until they were found innocent, unlike our similar procedure, which is radically different. You took away the dead man's papers, and have, it seems, returned for one which you missed. What was that paper?'

'Am I under examination?' said Mary Arnaud.

'No.'

'Then why do you assume all this against me? What right have you to do it? Be quiet until I send for my mother.'

Madame Mantalent was not long in coming. The Frenchwoman faced the Prussian as the Ophiophagus Elaps faces the Cobra. She, at all events, had never forgiven the advance of Blucher from Ligny to

Waterloo, though she had long ago forgiven the English, Scotch and Irish for standing in that rain of iron for so many hours, and, in fact, considered Wellington only inferior to Buonaparte and Moreau. She was nearly old enough to have heard of Rossbach. She faced the Prussian notary with what may be called, without disrespect, an evil eye.

'What have you been saying to my daughter?' she asked, stamping her stick upon the ground.

'I have been saying, madame, that your daughter has removed Mr. Drummond's papers before his death, and has carried them to England. She has represented herself as his sister, and now confesses that she is nothing of the kind; that under the Prussian law is what you call in England felony. We cannot disguise from ourselves, madame, that she has returned to seek a paper which she missed, and we must detain her.'

'Did the dead man,' said Madame Mantalent slowly, 'give her a receipt in full, witnessed by the doctor, for all the papers she took?'

'He certainly did,' said the doctor.

'We can produce the document,' said Madame Mantalent, 'but that is of very little matter. We *have* come back to recover a paper which belonged to the dead man, and which was certainly in his possession, as we know. Now, I want to ask you two scoundrels, you, Prussian notary, and you, quack English doctor, what you have done with it between you? I have more money than you two put together, and I will hunt you from one court to another. What have you done with it? You have not a leg to stand on. If my daughter was dishonest, would she have come back here to seek it? You have the paper between you, and if there was law in Prussia, I would make you give it up: but I will take uncommonly good care, doctor, to denounce you in England as a swindler.'

To say that Mrs. Arnaud was taken by surprise by her mother's flank movement is to say nothing. She had had so many surprises in this world that another was nothing to her. I am sorry to say about my very dear friend that she was pretending to weep behind her handkerchief, while she was choking with laughter, about the way in which her mother had turned the enemies' flank. She thought that the conclusion was the best.

'Gentlemen,' she said, rising and whisking her handkerchief. 'I am an old woman, near my grave. You have been tempted, doubtless, as many of us have, and you have yielded to temptation. I am a woman of business. You have the document I require here; I am rich, and I will give you a thousand sovereigns for it.'

And so she marched off to bed. The Englishman and the Prussian were no match for the old Frenchwoman. She had entirely beaten them, and the doctor only desired to get her out of the house. There was no more talk of arrest; and when Mrs. Arnaud was putting her mother to bed, she mildly remonstrated with her.

'Mamma, you went too far.'

'You can never do that, my dear. I have played the low insular game of cribbage, and if you peg too far you may be detected and have to go back; but you will find, if you raise a sufficient argument, that your adversary in the next hand will not play well, and so you gain in any way.'

'But, mamma, were you right in saying those dreadful things about them?'

'My dear, they have not got the paper. Besides, even if they had, I offered them a thousand pounds for it, and they neither of them had presence of mind to refuse. That in England would be twenty years' penal servitude for either of them. Their tongues are tied.

'I wonder where the paper is,' said Mrs. Arnaud.

CHAPTER XVIII.

ONE SMALL FLAME GOES OUT.

It is very painful for the present writer to speak of the fearful disasters which came down so suddenly on the most venerated head of Lord Festiniog. Of course, our moral readers will quarrel with us at once when we say that he was a good old fellow, and that there really was no harm in him. He wanted to possess the property, and he believed in the validity of a certain document, which was not worth the paper on which it was written.

He let the two women, Mrs. Arnaud and Madame Mantalent, go to St. Goar to see if they could recover it. That was extremely wrong. They made an utter failure, which served him right. Still, Nemesis punished him somewhat heavily; for the woman, Carlina, had taken the paper straight to Lord Rhyader, and before she had been with him half an hour, George Drummond had arrived from Marseilles.

Lord Rhyader—who was now in the House—was among pyramids of blue books. He was thinking about making a speech, which has never been made. He heard a rustle in his study, and swore under his breath. Seeing that it was only his valet, he kept his temper.

'An Italian woman wishes to see your lordship,' said the valet.

'Am I an organ-grinder man?' said Lord Rhyader, 'that you should talk to me of an Italian woman?'

'You had better see her, my lord. It is that woman, Carlina.'

'Oh, I see. Send her up.'

Up came the Italian woman, and went straight to the point. She told Lord Rhyader very much which he had guessed, but a great deal which he did not know. She pointed out that she had a certain paper in her possession, which deprived the Festiniog part of the family of all their inheritance, and gave it to the Killigrews.'

'May I see this paper?' he asked Carlina.

'No, my lord, it is in safer hands than mine.'

'You will give me time for deliberation, will you not?' said Lord Rhyader.

'I can only give you two hours,' said Carlina.

'I am all abroad over this matter,' said

Lord Rhyader. 'I wish for advice. Could you possibly meet me in two hours from this time, at No. 17 Hartley Street, Cavendish Square?'

Carlina hesitated, and looked at him. At last she said:—

'The English word is to be trusted. Will you swear to me, from being assassinated in that horrible house?'

Lord Rhyader gave his word to her. He said:—'I do not quite understand what you mean. No. 17 is pleasantly remembered by some of our family.'

'Your family are idiots,' she replied. 'Mrs. Arnaud, Madame Mantalent, Clotilde, and Heloise, are all Jesuits. Every one.'

'Well, my dear madam,' said Lord Rhyader, 'I will see you safe through your visit. Do not fail us.'

Lord Rhyader went at once to No. 17;

the door was opened by Rachel; he was shown into the back-parlour by Clotilde; and there sat, looking extremely tired and worn, George Drummond.

'Cousin George,' said Lord Rhyader, 'we all thought that you were drowned. We are very glad to find that it is not the case.'

'Cousin Rhyader,' said George Arnaud, 'it would have been better had I been drowned. I risked my life to save your boy. That is acknowledged?'

'Most fully,' my dear Arnaud. God knows how fully.'

'Have I omitted any duty to your family?'

'Certainly none.'

'Suppose I were to tell you that there was no family. That we were beggars and impostors, what would you do?'

'I suppose that the woman, Carlina, has been with you?' said Lord Rhyader.

'Well, she has.'

'What do you propose to do, George Arnaud?' said Lord Rhyader.

'Give up everything,' said George Arnaud. 'Put the thing in Chancery, and let the estate pay, if you like.'

'Quite my idea,' said Lord Rhyader. 'But my father, Lord Festiniog. What would he do?'

It was rather an alarming question, because Lord Festiniog happened to walk into the room at that moment; looking exactly as if nothing was the matter, whereas he perfectly well knew that a very great deal was the matter. He had heard of George Arnaud's arrival, and was very glad, apparently, to see him. He had something on his mind: something, which put everything else in the shade. The arrival of George Arnaud was nothing now.

'I am glad that you are here, sir,' said Lord Rhyader: 'there is this woman, Carlina, who seems to have a great deal more to do with our family than I like, coming; she, it seems, holds some deed, which utterly disinherits and ruins us. Do you know anything about it?'

'Yes, I do,' said Lord Festiniog. 'I encouraged Mary Arnaud and Madame Mantalent to go to Germany, and try to secure it.'

'Is the document of any value?' asked Lord Rhyader.

'Of the greatest value,' said Lord Festiniog. 'We are beggars without it. We must make terms with the woman, Rhyader, or we shall be in the workhouse.'

'Neither I, nor George Arnaud, will do

anything of the kind, sir. What relations have you made over this matter with Mrs. Arnaud and Madame Mantalent?'

'They were very brief, Rhyader. I think that I was not to blame very much. You should not be angry with me, just now.'

Lord Festiniog looked peculiarly troubled.

'You have,' said Lord Rhyader, 'entered into some compact with those two women about this Italian woman's paper. I and George Arnaud will have nothing to do with it. I, for my part, curse it.'

'Rhyader!' said Lord Festiniog, drawing himself up, 'do not curse your father's actions.'

'Why not, my lord?' said Lord Rhyader.

'Because you have no son left to curse your own. Barri died two hours ago.'

CHAPTER XIX.

TEMPTED ONCE TOO OFTEN.

'So Barri is dead!' said George Arnaud. I am most deeply sorry. I risked my life for him, and I could do no more. Lord Rhyader, you will bear me out in that fact.'

'Certainly. Barri dead? Yes! Well! God afflicts us sorely. Why, heaven help us, all the property would have gone to you, George Arnaud.'

'My dear Rhyader,' said Lord Festiniog, 'have you no other word to say when I tell you of the death of your son?'

'Everything which is affectionate I will

say or write down. But I fancy the boy is better out of the world than in it.'

'Why?' said Lord Festiniog.

'Because he would be a beggar like the rest of us. He will be an angel in heaven.'

'Do you mean to give up everything, sir?' said Lord Festiniog, turning on George Arnaud savagely. 'I ask you: do you mean to do it and retire once more into the original beggary from which you were rescued? Are you going to follow that ass, noodle, and prig of a son of mine in his curses, or are you going to behave like a man?'

'Let us come outside and talk, Lord Festiniog,' said George Arnaud.

They went out into the shop, among the dresses, and Lord Festiniog said:—

'My dear George Arnaud: I want to put a matter before you, and to put it without temper. I lost my temper just now, with my son, and I apologise for it. There is no doubt that your putative father was a great scoundrel, and that long after he was married he behaved very badly to your mother. Now, he got possession of a certain document, which would disinherit the whole of us, and the woman Carlina has it in her possession. Under these circumstances, I ask you, as a moral young man, what is to be done?'

George Arnaud, that most moral, excellent, and admirable young man, sat down in a chair in the shop at No. 17, and thought. At last he spoke.

'My lord,' he said, 'I have thought through the matter once more' (had he?) and I think that on the whole I would buy the document from the woman. I think that it would be best.'

Lord Festiniog spoke again.

'George Arnaud,' he said, 'do you see

this? Neither Rhyader nor myself will ever marry again. You will take my title and my estates without any dispute. It is in your interest that the paper should be got hold of and destroyed, as much as any one else's. Do you agree to its being done?'

'Rhyader might object.'

'Fudge,' said Lord Festiniog. 'I am not going to consult that noodle. You have got to decide whether you will be a beggar or a peer. I know that the woman is coming here directly. Say the word.

'Why does not your lordship say it yourself?'

'Because it is a matter of entire indifference to me, personally. There will be a grand lawsuit, but plenty of money to keep me comfortably. As for Rhyader, I don't care for him very much. I have liked you better lately. Come, decide.

'I would buy the paper of the woman then, my lord.'

Lord Festiniog was standing behind George Arnaud, and so he could not see the look of intense scorn which was on the lord's face. He said:

'It is felony, mind you, and you are concerned in it with me.'

George Arnaud said quietly, 'I am in good company, my lord.'

'Then we will both go to hell together,' said Lord Festiniog.

The speech startled George Arnaud for a moment. He had meant to be very pure over the matter, but he had changed his mind. With Lord Rhyader he was trying to do his duty; with Lord Festiniog he was prevented from doing it. Lord Festiniog—he, George Arnaud, was the future Lord Festiniog; and from the contemplation of that fact his morality suffered.

I do not wish to dwell on what happened almost immediately at No. 17. The Italian woman, Carlina, came with her paper, accompanied by her relatives, probably either bandits or organ-grinders: George Arnaud declares that they were the latter. She gave Lord Festiniog the paper, which was not worth a shilling, and he paid her one thousand pounds in bank notes. When she was gone, George Arnaud and he solemnly burnt that paper, and Lord Rhyader politely declined to know anything about the matter.

George Arnaud had been tempted once too often, and had fallen.

CHAPTER XX.

CONCLUSION.

I AM afraid that our story has been very immoral, and that every character in it, with the exception of the two young French ladies, Heloise and Clotilde, and of Lady Rhyader, ought to be picking oakum in Coldbath Fields. The writer has not a single word to say for any one of them, except that he likes them, as some people have been known to love extremely naughty children of either sex.

It is possible, however, that the reader may like to hear how the judgments of Nemesis overtook the gang of miscreants of which the writer has attempted to give a sketch. Although they were all engaged more or less in a misprision of felony, no remarkable judgments overtook them.

Madam Mantalent's rheumatism and obstinacy caused her to remain in Paris during the siege, where it has been affirmed that she ate her cat. That is totally untrue, because her cat is at No. 17 to this day. What became of Mrs. Arnaud's pet colly dog, who certainly went into Paris, and equally certainly never came out again, we don't know. Since the Commune business, Madame Mantalent has settled in England permanently, as she intended to do several times before. Her conversation is charming, but she objects to any mention of the siege of Paris, unless she has all the conversation to herself.

She says that the behaviour of the

Germans was extremely odious, but that all the Germans in creation were less detestable than Madame Virmesch: who induced her husband to ruin trade in Paris. She says that M. Virmesch was a '*bon garçon*' ruined by his wife. The Communists, she adds, had no taste for colour. The red, which they so abundantly used, was extremely raw, and by no means of the right tint. When madame is examined on the subject of French politics, she is rather puzzling. She is not Cæsarist, because she says that the lady of Chislehurst had never any taste in ribands, though she was in other ways a most admirable lady. 'What,' says Madame Mantalent, 'are you to do with a great lady who wears round her neck English eau de Nile from Coventry?' In fact, Madame Mantalent has quarrelled with the Imperial family on the subject of dress. She has also had a few very decisive words with Madame MacMahon on the same subject; and Madame Mac Mahon has had to yield, at least so it is said. Mrs. Grant's head-dress was reported to her correspondent as being objectionable: she at once wrote to the President of the United States. Nay, more: our own Queen had on one day a bonnet, which, as Madame Mantalent thought, did not suit her; and Madame Mantalent at once wrote off to say that she would be glad of an interview. It was not granted, and No 17 remained without royal patronage.

But No. 17 flourished strangely. There was a curious atmosphere about it which attracted certain people. There was no one ever came there who was not in some sense a sinner, but then, who is blameless? The people who came there were people who were tired of the world, and who were waiting for death. They had all of them more money than they knew how to dispose of; but they were tired of the world, and wished to be out of it. Lord Rhyader expressed this opinion first, and Lord Festiniog rebuked him, but Mary Arnaud and Madame Mantalent backed him up.

'Why need we live?' said Mrs. Arnaud, 'I have lived three lives, and I am tired.'

'Why were we ever born,' said Madame Mantalent? 'For art? Nonsense. For politics? Once more nonsense, To reproduce ourselves? Again nonsense. There is my daughter, is she in any way worthy of me?—Yes my darling, you are worth fifty of me. Don't mind the old woman. How much happier we shall be when we are dead!'

Lord Festiniog was not certain about that.

He considered that we did not know enough about the next world.

George Arnaud backed Lord Festiniog; and the conversation changed, although from time to time it was renewed for some few years.

Lord Rhyader was, singularly enough, the first to go. He took to his bed, stayed there, and died. His last words were very solemnly spoken. 'Giraldus Cambrensis,' he said, 'was the founder of our house. He was a churchman, and I want no scandal in the family, but I would sooner have the bar sinister on our arms than deny the fact. He was head of the Barris. As for the Irish Barrys—there—' Those were his lordship's last words.

It was some time before Madame Mantalent went that Clotilde took the veil. D'Arcy had come into a great deal of money, and he and Heloise were spinning about in the world like a couple of teetotums. Madame Mantalent, as D'Arcy and his wife averred, had asked Lord Festiniog to marry her, and his lordship had declined, though with the greatest politeness; urging age, which madam said was of no consequence at all.

However, they were not married, and Madame Mantalent died. In reality she was killed by her rheumatism, but she declared that her death blow came from seeing a great lady in blue silk with rubies. 'Whatever you may say of the Buonapartists, they would never have done *that.*' And so she closed her eyes and never opened them any more. We fancy after all that she died in the Buonapartist faith; and in the end only a very high Catholic. There are many worse old women in the world than Madame Mantalent, when all is said and done, though the present writer would much rather be her biographer than her spiritual director.

We were in Westminister Hall a few days ago, when we saw a woman in deep mourning talking to a very tall young man. Both of them had their backs towards us, but I was perfectly certain that there were not three women in England who could carry themselves in the way of the lady in mourning. We approached, and they turned; we saw before us Mrs. Arnaud and a young gentleman, tall, gaunt and melancholy, whom we did not recognize,—a man with a large beard, ill-trimmed, with a bronzed face, a man who frowned at you but did not scowl.

'My dear Sir,' said Mrs. Arnaud, 'I

want to get into the House of Commons, can you tell me any one who would help me? My son says that it is difficult to-night; let me introduce you. My son, Lord Festiniog.'

'Lord Festiniog?' I said. 'You don't mean to say that the dear old man is dead? I have been in Scotland, and have never heard of it.'

We went into a recess between the Hall and the lobby of the House of Commons, and she told us of it. The old fellow had died in his chair one morning, and his last words had been, 'Divine Providence is mysterious, when it permits the increase of the human race. What does it all mean? Merely misery, sorrow, and sin. Now I am going to be happy.'

Lord Festiniog, whilome George Drummond, came up, took his mother's arm, and led her away. 'You will make an excellent peer,' thought we, 'but I liked the dear old fellow better than I shall ever like you.'

END OF THE SECOND VOLUME.

LONDON: PRINTED BY
SPOTTISWOODE AND CO., NEW-STREET SQUARE
AND PARLIAMENT STREET

A List of Books

PUBLISHED BY

CHATTO & WINDUS

74 & 75, *PICCADILLY, LONDON, W.*

ADVERTISING, A HISTORY OF, from the Earliest Times. Illustrated by Anecdotes, Curious Specimens, and Biographical Notes of Successful Advertisers. By HENRY SAMPSON. Crown 8vo, with Coloured Frontispiece and Illustrations, cloth gilt, 7*s.* 6*d.*

ÆSOP'S FABLES TRANSLATED INTO HUMAN NATURE. By C. H. BENNETT. Crown 4to, 24 Plates beautifully printed in Colours, with descriptive Text, cloth extra, gilt, 6*s.*

"For fun and frolic the new version of Æsop's Fables must bear away the palm. There are twenty-two fables and twenty-two wonderful coloured illustrations; the moral is pointed, the tale adorned. This is not a juvenile book, but there are plenty of grown-up children who like to be amused at Christmas, and indeed at any time of the year; and if this new version of old stories does not amuse them they must be very dull indeed, and their situation one much to be commiserated."—*Morning Post.*

AINSWORTH'S LATIN DICTIONARY. The only Modern Edition which comprises the Complete Work. With numerous Additions, Emendations, and Improvements, by the Rev. B. W. BEATSON and W. ELLIS. Imperial 8vo, cloth extra, 15*s.*

AMUSING POETRY. A Selection from the Best Writers. Edited, with Preface, by SHIRLEY BROOKS. Fcap. 8vo, cloth, gilt edges, 3*s.* 6*d.*

ANACREON. Translated by THOMAS MOORE, and Illustrated by the exquisite Designs of GIRODET. Oblong 8vo, Etruscan gold and blue, 12*s.* 6*d.*

ARTEMUS WARD, COMPLETE.—The Works of CHARLES FARRER BROWNE, better known as ARTEMUS WARD. With fine Portrait, facsimile of Handwriting, &c. Crown 8vo, cloth extra, 7*s.* 6*d.*

AS PRETTY AS SEVEN, and other Popular German Stories. Collected by LUDWIG BECHSTEIN. With Additional Tales by the Brothers GRIMM, and 100 Illustrations by RICHTER. Small 4to, green and gold, 6*s.* 6*d.*; gilt edges, 7*s.* 6*d.*

ASTLE ON WRITING.—THE ORIGIN AND PROGRESS OF WRITING, as well Hieroglyphic as Elementary, Illustrated by Engravings taken from Marbles, Manuscripts, and Charters, Ancient and Modern; also Some Account of the Origin and Progress of Printing. By THOMAS ASTLE, F.R.S., F.A.S., late Keeper of Records in the Tower of London. Royal 4to, half-Roxburghe, with 33 Plates (some Coloured), price £1 15*s*. A few Large Paper copies, royal folio, half-Roxburghe, the Plates altogether unfolded, price £3 3*s*.

BACON'S (Francis, Lord) WORKS, both English and Latin, with an Introductory Essay, Biographical and Critical, and copious Indexes. Two Vols., imperial 8vo, with Portrait, cloth extra, £1 4*s*.

BANKERS, A HANDBOOK OF LONDON; with some Account of their Predecessors, the Early Goldsmiths, together with Lists of Bankers, from the Earliest London Directory printed in 1677, to the Official List of 1875. By F. G. HILTON PRICE. Crown 8vo, cloth extra, 7*s*. 6*d*. [*In the press.*

BARDSLEY'S OUR ENGLISH SURNAMES: Their Sources and Significations. By CHARLES WAREING BARDSLEY, M.A. SECOND EDITION, revised throughout, considerably Enlarged, and partially rewritten. Crown 8vo, cloth extra, 9*s*.

"Mr. Bardsley has faithfully consulted the original mediæval documents and works from which the origin and development of surnames can alone be satisfactorily traced. He has furnished a valuable contribution to the literature of surnames, and we hope to hear more of him in this field."—*Times*.

BAUER AND HOOKER'S GENERA OF FERNS; in which the Characters of each Genus are displayed in a series of magnified dissections and figures, highly finished in colours, after the drawings of FRANCIS BAUER, with letterpress by Sir WILLIAM HOOKER. Imperial 8vo, with 120 beautifully Coloured Plates, half-morocco, gilt, £5 5*s*.

BEAUTIFUL PICTURES BY BRITISH ARTISTS: A Gathering of Favourites from our Picture Galleries. In Two Series. The FIRST SERIES including Examples by WILKIE, CONSTABLE, TURNER, MULREADY LANDSEER, MACLISE, E. M. WARD, FRITH, Sir JOHN GILBERT, LESLIE, ANSDELL, MARCUS STONE, Sir NOEL PATON, FAED, EYRE CROWE, GAVIN, O'NEIL, and MADOX BROWN. The SECOND containing Pictures by ARMYTAGE, FAED, GOODALL, HEMSLEY, HORSLEY, MARKS, NICHOLLS, Sir NOEL PATON, PICKERSGILL, G. SMITH, MARCUS STONE, SOLOMON, STRAIGHT, E. M. WARD, and WARREN. All engraved on Steel in the highest style of Art. Edited, with Notices of the Artists, by SYDNEY ARMYTAGE, M.A. Price of each Series, imperial 4to, cloth extra, gilt and gilt edges, 21*s*. *Each Volume is Complete in itself.*

BELL'S (Sir Charles) ANATOMY OF EXPRESSION, as connected with the Fine Arts. Fifth Edition, with an Appendix on the Nervous System by ALEXANDER SHAW. Illustrated with 45 beautiful Engravings. Imp. 8vo, cloth extra, gilt, 16*s*.

BINGHAM'S ANTIQUITIES of the CHRISTIAN CHURCH. A New Edition, revised, with copious Index. Two Vols., imperial 8vo, cloth extra, £1 4*s*.

"A writer who does equal honour to the English clergy and to the English nation, and whose learning is to be equalled only by his moderation and impartiality."—*Quarterly Review*.

BIOGRAPHICAL AND CRITICAL DICTIONARY OF RECENT AND LIVING PAINTERS AND ENGRAVERS, both English and Foreign. By HENRY OTTLEY. Being a Supplementary Volume to "Bryan's Dictionary." Imperial 8vo, cloth extra, 12*s*.

*** *This is the only work giving an account of the principal living painters of all countries.*

BLAKE'S WORKS.—A Series of Reproductions in Facsimile of the Works of WILLIAM BLAKE, including the "Songs of Innocence and Experience," "The Book of Thel," "America," "The Vision of the Daughters of Albion," "The Marriage of Heaven and Hell," "Europe, a Prophecy," "Jerusalem," "Milton," "Urizen," "The Song of Los," &c. These Works will be issued both coloured and plain. [*In preparation.*

"Blake is a real name, I assure you, and a most extraordinary man he is, if he still be living. He is the Blake whose wild designs accompany a splendid edition of Blair's 'Grave.' He paints in water-colours marvellous strange pictures—visions of his brain—which he asserts he has seen. They have great merit. I must look upon him as one of the most extraordinary persons of the age."—CHARLES LAMB.

BLANCHARD'S (Laman) POEMS. Now first Collected. Edited, with a Life of the Author (including numerous hitherto unpublished Letters from Lord LYTTON, LAMB, DICKENS, ROBERT BROWNING, and others), by BLANCHARD JERROLD. Crown 8vo, cloth extra. [*In preparation.*

BOCCACCIO'S DECAMERON; or, Ten Days' Entertainment. Translated into English, with Introduction by THOMAS WRIGHT, Esq., M.A., F.S.A. With Portrait after RAPHAEL, and STOTHARD'S beautiful Copperplates. Crown 8vo, cloth extra, gilt, 7*s.* 6*d.*

BOLTON'S SONG BIRDS OF GREAT BRITAIN. Illustrated with Figures, the size of Life, of both Male and Female; of their Nests and Eggs, Food, Favourite Plants, Shrubs, Trees, &c. &c. Two Vols. in One, royal 4to containing 80 beautifully Coloured Plates, half-Roxburghe, £3 13*s.* 6*d.*

BOOKSELLERS, A HISTORY OF. Including the Story of the Rise and Progress of the Great Publishing Houses, in London and the Provinces, and of their greatest Works. By HARRY CURWEN. Crown 8vo, with Frontispiece and numerous Portraits and Illustrations, cloth extra, 7*s.* 6*d.*

"In these days, ten ordinary Histories of Kings and Courtiers were well exchanged against the tenth part of one good History of Booksellers."—THOMAS CARLYLE.

"This stout little book is unquestionably amusing. Ill-starred, indeed, must be the reader who, opening it anywhere, lights upon six consecutive pages within the entire compass of which some good anecdote or smart repartee is not to be found."—*Saturday Review.*

BOUDOIR BALLADS: Vers de Société. By J. ASHBY STERRY. Crown 8vo, cloth extra. [*In preparation.*

BRAND'S OBSERVATIONS ON POPULAR ANTIQUITIES, chiefly Illustrating the Origin of our Vulgar Customs, Ceremonies, and Superstitions. Arranged and revised, with Additions, by Sir HENRY ELLIS. A New Edition, with fine full-page Illustrations. Crown 8vo, cloth extra, gilt, 7*s.* 6*d.* [*In the press.*

BRET HARTE'S CHOICE WORKS in Prose and Poetry. With Introductory Essay by J. M. BELLEW, Portrait of the Author, and 50 Illustrations. Crown 8vo, cloth extra, 7*s.* 6*d.*

BREWSTER'S (Sir David) MARTYRS OF SCIENCE. A New Edition, in small crown 8vo, cloth extra, gilt, with full-page Portraits, 4*s.* 6*d.*

BREWSTER'S (Sir David) MORE WORLDS THAN ONE, the Creed of the Philosopher and the Hope of the Christian. A New Edition, in small crown 8vo, cloth extra, gilt, with full-page Astronomical Plates, 4*s.* 6*d.*

BRIC-À-BRAC HUNTER (The); or, Chapters on Chinamania. By Major H. BYNG HALL. With Photographic Frontispiece. Crown 8vo, cloth, full gilt (from a special and novel design), 10*s.* 6*d.*

BRITISH ESSAYISTS (The): viz., "Spectator," "Tatler," "Guardian," "Rambler," "Adventurer," "Idler," and "Connoisseur." Complete in Three thick Vols., 8vo with Portrait, cloth extra, £1 7*s.*

BROADSTONE HALL, and other Poems. By W. E. WINDUS. With 40 Illustrations by ALFRED CONCANEN. Crown 8vo, cloth extra, gilt, 5s.

"This little volume of poems is illustrated with such vigour, and shows such a thoroughly practical knowledge of and love for sea-life, that it is quite tonic and refreshing. Maudlin sentimentality is carefully eschewed, and a robust, manly tone of thought gives muscle to the verse and elasticity of mind to the reader."—*Morning Post.*

BROCKEDON'S PASSES OF THE ALPS. Containing 109 fine Engravings by FINDEN, WILLMORE, and others; with Maps of each Pass, and a General Map of the Alps by ARROWSMITH. Two Vols., 4to, half-bound morocco, gilt edges, £3 13s. 6d.

BULWER'S (Lytton) PILGRIMS OF THE RHINE. With Portrait and 27 exquisite Line Engravings on Steel, by GOODALL, WILLMORE, and others; after Drawings by DAVID ROBERTS and MACLISE. Crown 8vo, cloth extra, top edges gilt, 10s. 6d.

BUNYAN'S PILGRIM'S PROGRESS. Edited by Rev. T. SCOTT. With 17 beautiful Steel Plates by STOTHARD, engraved by GOODALL; and numerous Woodcuts. Crown 8vo, cloth extra, gilt, 7s. 6d.

BURNET'S HISTORY OF HIS OWN TIME, from the Restoration of Charles II. to the Treaty of Peace at Utrecht. With Historical and Biographical Notes and copious Index. Imp. 8vo, with Portrait, cloth extra, 13s. 6d.

BURNET'S HISTORY OF THE REFORMATION OF THE CHURCH OF ENGLAND. A New Edition, with numerous illustrative Notes and copious Index. Two Vols., imperial 8vo, cloth extra, £1 1s.

BYRON'S (Lord) LETTERS AND JOURNALS. With Notices of his Life. By THOMAS MOORE. A Reprint of the Original Edition, newly revised, complete in a thick Volume of 1060 pp., with Twelve full-page Plates. Crown 8vo, cloth extra, gilt, 7s. 6d.

"We have read this book with the greatest pleasure. Considered merely as a composition, it deserves to be classed among the best specimens of English prose which our age has produced. . . . The style is agreeable, clear, and manly, and, when it rises into eloquence, rises without effort or ostentation. Nor is the matter inferior to the manner. It would be difficult to name a book which exhibits more kindness, fairness, and modesty."—MACAULAY, in the *Edinburgh Review.*

CALMET'S BIBLE DICTIONARY. Edited by CHARLES TAYLOR. With the Fragments incorporated and arranged in Alphabetical Order. New Edition. Imperial 8vo, with Maps and Wood Engravings, cloth extra, 10s. 6d.

CANOVA'S WORKS IN SCULPTURE AND MODELLING. 150 Plates, exquisitely engraved in Outline by MOSES, and printed on an India tint. With Descriptions by the Countess ALBRIZZI, a Biographical Memoir by CICOGNARA, and Portrait by WORTHINGTON. A New Edition. Demy 4to, cloth extra, gilt, gilt edges, 31s. 6d. [*In the press.*

CARLYLE (Thomas) ON THE CHOICE OF BOOKS. With New Life and Anecdotes. Small post 8vo, brown cloth, 1s. 6d.

CAROLS OF COCKAYNE; Vers de Société descriptive of London Life. By HENRY S. LEIGH. Third Edition. With numerous Illustrations by ALFRED CONCANEN. Crown 8vo, cloth extra, gilt, 5s.

CARTER'S ANCIENT ARCHITECTURE OF ENGLAND. Including the Orders during the British, Roman, Saxon, and Norman Eras; and also under the Reigns of Henry III. and Edward III. Illustrated by 103 large Copperplate Engravings, comprising upwards of Two Thousand Specimens. Edited by JOHN BRITTON. Royal folio, half-morocco extra, £2 8s.

*** *This national work on ancient architecture occupied its author, in drawing tching, arranging, and publishing, more than twenty years, and he himself declared it to be the result of his studies through life.*

CARTER'S ANCIENT SCULPTURE NOW REMAINING IN ENGLAND, from the Earliest Period to the Reign of Henry VIII.; consisting of Statues, Basso-relievos, Sculptures, &c., Brasses, Monumental Effigies, Paintings on Glass and on Walls; Missal Ornaments; Carvings on Cups, Croziers, Chests, Seals; Ancient Furniture, &c. &c. With Historical and Critical Illustrations by DOUCE, MEYRICK, DAWSON TURNER, and JOHN BRITTON. Royal folio, with 120 large Engravings, many Illuminated, half-bound morocco extra, £8 8*s*.

CATLIN'S ILLUSTRATIONS OF THE MANNERS, CUSTOMS, AND CONDITION OF THE NORTH AMERICAN INDIANS, written during Eight Years of Travel and Adventure among the Wildest and most Remarkable Tribes now existing. Containing 360 Coloured Engravings from the Author's original Paintings. Two Vols., imperial 8vo, Cloth extra, gilt, the Plates beautifully printed in Colours, £1 10*s*.

"One of the most admirable observers of manners who ever lived among the aborigines of America."—HUMBOLDT's *Cosmos*.

CATLIN'S NORTH AMERICAN INDIAN PORTFOLIO. Containing Hunting Scenes, Amusements, Scenery, and Costume of the Indians of the Rocky Mountains and Prairies of America, from Drawings and Notes made by the Author during Eight Years' Travel. A series of 31 magnificent Plates, beautifully coloured in facsimile of the Original Drawings exhibited at the Egyptian Hall. With Letterpress Descriptions, imperial folio, half-morocco, gilt, £7 10*s*.

*** *Five of the above Drawings are now for the first time published.*

CHAMBERLAINE'S IMITATIONS OF DRAWINGS FROM THE GREAT MASTERS in the Royal Collection. Engraved by BARTOLOZZI and others. 74 fine Plates, mostly tinted; including, in addition, "Ecce Homo," after GUIDO, and the scarce Series of 7 Anatomical Drawings. Imperial folio, half-morocco, gilt edges, £5 5*s*.

CHATTO'S (W. Andrew) HISTORY OF WOOD ENGRAVING, Historical and Practical. A New Edition, with an Additional Chapter. Illustrated by 445 fine Wood Engravings. Imperial 8vo, half-Roxburghe, £2 2*s*.

"This volume is one of the most interesting and valuable of modern times."—*Art Union.*

CHRISTMAS CAROLS AND BALLADS. Selected and Edited by JOSHUA SYLVESTER. Cloth extra, gilt, gilt edges, 3*s*. 6*d*.

CICERO'S FAMILIAR LETTERS, AND LETTERS TO ATTICUS. Translated by MELMOTH and HEBERDEN. With Life of Cicero by MIDDLETON. Royal 8vo, with Portrait, cloth extra, 12*s*.

"Cicero is the type of a perfect letter-writer, never boring you with moral essays out of season, always evincing his mastery over his art by the most careful consideration for your patience and amusement. We should rifle the volumes of antiquity in vain to find a letter-writer who converses on paper so naturally, so engagingly, so much from the heart as Cicero."—*Quarterly Review.*

CLAUDE'S LIBER VERITATIS. A Collection of 303 Prints after the Original Designs of CLAUDE. Engraved by RICHARD EARLOM. With a descriptive Catalogue of each Print, Lists of the Persons for whom, and the Places for which, the original Pictures were first painted, and of the present Possessors of most of them. London: published by Messrs. Boydell and Co., Cheapside. Printed by W. Bulmer and Co., Cleveland Row, 1777. Three Vols. folio, half-morocco extra, gilt edges, £10 10*s*.

CLAUDE, BEAUTIES OF, containing 24 of his choicest Landscapes, beautifully Engraved on Steel, by BROMLEY, LUPTON, and others. With Biographical Sketch and Portrait. Royal folio, in a portfolio, £1 5*s*.

COLLINS' (Wilkie) NOVELS. New Illustrated Library Editions, price 6*s.* each, with Frontispiece and several full-page Illustrations in each Volume:—

The Woman in White. Illustrated by Sir JOHN GILBERT and F. A. FRASER.

Antonina; or, The Fall of Rome. Illustrated by Sir JOHN GILBERT and ALFRED CONCANEN.

Basil. Illustrated by Sir JOHN GILBERT and M. F. MAHONEY.

The Dead Secret. Illustrated by Sir JOHN GILBERT and H. FURNISS.

The Queen of Hearts. Illustrated by Sir JOHN GILBERT and ALFRED CONCANEN.

The Moonstone. Illustrated by G. DU MAURIER and F. A. FRASER.

Man and Wife. Illustrated by WILLIAM SMALL.

Hide and Seek; or, The Mystery of Mary Grice. Illustrated by Sir JOHN GILBERT and M. F. MAHONEY.

Poor Miss Finch. Illustrated by GEORGE DU MAURIER and EDWARD HUGHES.

Miss or Mrs.? Illustrated by S. L. FILDES and HENRY WOODS.

The New Magdalen. With Illustrations by GEO. DU MAURIER and C. S. R.

The Frozen Deep. Illustrated by G. DU MAURIER and M. F. MAHONEY.

My Miscellanies. With Steel-plate Portrait of the Author, and Illustrations by ALFRED CONCANEN.

COLLINS' (Wilkie) THE LAW AND THE LADY. Three Vols., crown 8vo, 31*s.* 6*d.*

"*Edwin.* Read any novels lately?—*Angelina.* Just read an awfully nice book, 'The Law and the Lady.' One of the heroes is a monstrosity without legs, 'Miserrimus Dexter,' don't you know. Awfully clever.—*Edwin.* O yes. Read the book myself. Clever notion, the idiotic man-woman, eh, wasn't it?—*Angelina.* O yes, awfully good."—*Punch.*

"An exceedingly clever novel, full of admirable writing, abounding in a subtle ingenuity which is a distinct order of genius. . . . . 'The Law and the Lady' will be read with avidity by all who delight in the romances of the greatest master the sensational novel has ever known."—*World.*

COLMAN'S HUMOROUS WORKS.—Broad Grins, My Nightgown and Slippers, and other Humorous Works, Prose and Poetical, of GEORGE COLMAN. With Life and Anecdotes by G. B. BUCKSTONE, and Frontispiece by HOGARTH. Crown 8vo, cloth extra, gilt, 7*s.* 6*d.*

CONEY'S ENGRAVINGS OF ANCIENT CATHEDRALS, Hôtels de Ville, Town Halls, &c., including some of the finest Examples of Gothic Architecture in France, Holland, Germany, and Italy. 32 large Plates, imperial folio, half-morocco extra, £3 13*s.* 6*d.*

CONQUEST OF THE SEA (The). A History of Diving from the Earliest Times. By HENRY SIEBE. Profusely Illustrated. Crown 8vo, cloth extra, gilt, 4*s.* 6*d.*

"We have perused this volume, full of quaint information, with delight. Mr. Siebe has bestowed much pains on his work; he writes with enthusiasm and fulness of knowledge."—*Echo.*

"Really interesting alike to youths and to grown-up people."—*Scotsman.*

CONSTABLE'S GRAPHIC WORKS. Comprising 40 highly finished Mezzotinto Engravings on Steel, by DAVID LUCAS; with descriptive Letterpress by C. R. LESLIE, R.A. Folio, half-morocco, gilt edges, £2 2*s.*

COTMAN'S ENGRAVINGS OF THE SEPULCHRAL BRASSES IN NORFOLK AND SUFFOLK. With Letterpress Descriptions, an Essay on Sepulchral Memorials by DAWSON TURNER, Notes by Sir SAMUEL MEYRICK, ALBERT WAY, and Sir HARRIS NICOLAS, and copious Index. New Edition, containing 173 Plates, two of them splendidly Illuminated. Two Volumes, small folio, half-morocco extra, £6 6*s.*

COTMAN'S ETCHINGS OF ARCHITECTURAL REMAINS, chiefly Norman and Gothic, in various Counties in England, but principally in Norfolk, with Descriptive Notices by DAWSON TURNER, and Architectural Observations by THOMAS RICKMAN. Two Vols., imperial folio, containing 240 spirited Etchings, half-morocco, top edges gilt, £8 8*s.*

COTMAN'S LIBER STUDIORUM. A Series of Landscape Studies and Original Compositions, for the Use of Art Students, consisting of 48 Etchings, the greater part executed in "soft ground." Imperial folio, half-morocco, £1 11*s.* 6*d.*

COWPER'S POETICAL WORKS. Including his Translation of HOMER. Edited by the Rev. H. F. CARY. With Portrait and 18 Steel Engravings after HARVEY. Royal 8vo, cloth extra, gilt edges, 10*s.* 6*d.*

"I long to know your opinion of Cowper's Translation. The *Odyssey* especially is surely very Homeric. What nobler than the appearance of Phœbus at the beginning of the *Iliad*—lines ending with 'Dread sounding-bounding in the silver bow'?"—CHARLES LAMB, *in a Letter to Coleridge.*

CREASY'S MEMOIRS OF EMINENT ETONIANS; with Notices of the Early History of Eton College. By Sir EDWARD CREASY, Author of "The Fifteen Decisive Battles of the World." A New Edition, brought down to the Present Time, with Illustrations. Crown 8vo, cloth extra. [*In the press.*

CRUIKSHANK AT HOME. Tales and Sketches by the most Popular Authors. With numerous Illustrations by ROBERT CRUIKSHANK and ROBERT SEYMOUR. Also, CRUIKSHANK'S ODD VOLUME, or Book of Variety, Illustrated by Two Odd Fellows—SEYMOUR and CRUIKSHANK. Four Vols. bound in Two, fcap. 8vo, cloth extra, gilt, 10*s.* 6*d.*

CRUIKSHANK'S COMIC ALMANACK. Complete in Two SERIES: The FIRST from 1835 to 1843; the SECOND from 1844 to 1853. A Gathering of the BEST HUMOUR of THACKERAY, HOOD, MAYHEW, ALBERT SMITH, A'BECKETT, ROBERT BROUGH, &c. With 2000 Woodcuts and Steel Engravings by CRUIKSHANK, HINE, LANDELLS, &c. Crown 8vo, cloth gilt, two very thick volumes, 15*s.*; or, separately, 7*s.* 6*d.* per volume.

CRUIKSHANK'S UNIVERSAL SONGSTER. The largest Collection extant of the best Old English Songs (upwards of 5000). With 8 Engravings on Steel and Wood by GEORGE and R. CRUIKSHANK, and 8 Portraits. Three Vols., 8vo, cloth extra, gilt, 21*s.*

CUSSANS' HANDBOOK OF HERALDRY. With Instructions for Tracing Pedigrees and Deciphering Ancient MSS.; Rules for the Appointment of Liveries, Chapters on Continental and American Heraldry, &c. &c. By JOHN E. CUSSANS. Illustrated with 360 Plates and Woodcuts. Crown 8vo, cloth extra, gilt and emblazoned, 7*s.* 6*d.*

CUSSANS' HISTORY OF HERTFORDSHIRE. A County History, got up in a very superior manner, and ranging with the finest works of its class. By JOHN E. CUSSANS. Illustrated with full-page Plates on Copper and Stone, and a profusion of small Woodcuts. Parts I. to VIII. now ready, 21*s.* each.

**** An entirely new History of this important County, great attention being given to all matters pertaining to Family History.*

CUVIER'S ANIMAL KINGDOM, arranged after its Organization: forming a Natural History of Animals, and an Introduction to Comparative Anatomy. New Edition, with considerable Additions by W. B. CARPENTER and J. O. WESTWOOD. Illustrated by many Hundred Wood Engravings, and numerous Steel Engravings by THOS. LANDSEER, mostly Coloured. Imperial 8vo, cloth extra, 18*s.*

CYCLOPÆDIA OF COSTUME; or, A Dictionary of Dress—Regal, Ecclesiastical, Civil, and Military—from the Earliest Period in England to the reign of George the Third. Including Notices of Contemporaneous Fashions on the Continent, and preceded by a General History of the Costumes of the Principal Countries of Europe. By J. R. PLANCHÉ, Somerset Herald. To be Completed in Twenty-four Parts, quarto, at Five Shillings each, profusely illustrated by Coloured and Plain Plates and Wood Engravings.—A Prospectus will be sent upon application. [*In course of publication.*

"There is no subject connected with dress with which 'Somerset Herald' is not as familiar as ordinary men are with the ordinary themes of everyday life. The gathered knowledge of many years is placed before the world in this his latest work, and when finished, there will exist no work on the subject half so valuable. The numerous illustrations are all effective—for their accuracy the author is responsible; they are well drawn and well engraved, and, while indispensable to a proper comprehension of the text, are satisfactory as works of art."—*Art Journal.*

"These, the first numbers of a Cyclopædia of Ancient and Modern Costume, give promise that the work, when complete, will be one of the most perfect works ever published upon the subject. The illustrations are numerous and excellent, and would, even without the letterpress, render the work an invaluable book of reference for information as to costumes for fancy balls and character quadrilles."—*Standard.*

"Destined, we anticipate, to be the standard English work on dress."—*Builder.*

"Promises to be a very complete work on a subject of the greatest importance to the historian and the archæologist."—*Tablet.*

"Beautifully printed and superbly illustrated."—*Standard*, second notice.

D'ARBLAY'S (Madame) DIARY AND LETTERS. Edited by her Niece, CHARLOTTE BARRETT. A New Edition, in Four Vols., 8vo. Illustrated by numerous fine Portraits engraved on Steel. [*In the press.*

DIBDIN'S (T. F.) BIBLIOMANIA; or, Book-Madness: A Bibliographical Romance. With numerous Illustrations. A New Edition, with a Supplement, including a Key to the Assumed Characters in the Drama. Demy 8vo, half-Roxburghe, 21*s.*; a few Large Paper copies, half-Roxburghe, the edges altogether uncut, at 42*s.* [*In the press.*

DICKENS' LIFE AND SPEECHES. Royal 16mo, cloth extra, 2*s.* 6*d*

DISCOUNT TABLES, on a new and simple plan; to facilitate the Discounting of Bills, and the Calculation of Interest on Banking and Current Accounts, &c.; showing, without calculation, the number of days from every day in the year to any other day. By THOMAS READER. Post 8vo, cloth extra, 7*s.*

DIXON'S (Hepworth) NEW WORK.—WHITE CONQUEST: AMERICA IN 1875. 2 vols. demy 8vo, cloth extra, 30*s.* [*In the press.*

DON QUIXOTE: A Revised Translation, based upon those of MOTTEUX, JARVIS, and SMOLLETT. With 50 Illustrations by ARMSTRONG and TONY JOHANNOT. Royal 8vo, cloth extra, gilt, 10*s.* 6*d.*

DON QUIXOTE IN SPANISH.—EL INGENIOSO HIDALGO DON QUIJOTE DE LA MANCHA. Nueva Edicion, corregida y revisada. Por MIGUEL DE CERVANTES SAAVEDRA. Complete in One Volume, post 8vo, nearly 700 pages, cloth extra, price 4*s.* 6*d.*

DRURY'S ILLUSTRATIONS of FOREIGN ENTOMOLOGY. Containing, in 150 beautifully Coloured Plates, upwards of 600 Exotic Insects of the East and West Indies, China, New Holland, North and South America, Germany, &c. With important Additions and Scientific Indexes, by J. O. WESTWOOD, F.L.S. Three Vols., 4to, half-morocco extra, £5 5*s.*

DULWICH GALLERY (The): A Series of 50 beautifully Coloured Plates, from the most celebrated Pictures in this Collection, executed by the Custodian, R. COCKBURN, and mounted upon Cardboard, in the manner of Drawings. Imperial folio, in portfolio, £16 16*s.*

DUNLOP'S HISTORY OF FICTION: Being a Critical and Analytical Account of the most celebrated Prose Works of Fiction, from the Earliest Greek Romances to the Novels of the Present Day, with General Index. Third Edition, royal 8vo, cloth extra, 9*s.*

DUNRAVEN'S (The Earl of) THE GREAT DIVIDE: A Narrative of Travels in the Upper Yellowstone in the Summer of 1874. With numerous striking full-page Illustrations by VALENTINE W. BROMLEY. Demy 8vo, cloth extra, with Maps and Illustrations. [*In the press.*

EARLY ENGLISH POETS. A New Series is in preparation, Edited, with Introductions and copious Notes, by the Rev. A. B. GROSART. The following are in the press:—THE COMPLETE WORKS OF GILES FLETCHER, B.D.—THE WORKS OF SIR JOHN DAVIES.—THE WORKS OF SIR PHILIP SIDNEY.

ELLIS'S (Mrs.) MOTHERS OF GREAT MEN. A New Edition, with Illustrations by VALENTINE BROMLEY. Crown 8vo, cloth gilt, 6*s.*

EMANUEL ON DIAMONDS AND PRECIOUS STONES; Their History, Value, and Properties; with Simple Tests for ascertaining their Reality. By HARRY EMANUEL, F.R.G.S. With numerous Illustrations, Tinted and Plain. A New Edition, crown 8vo, cloth extra, gilt, 6*s.*

ENGLISHMAN'S HOUSE (The): A Practical Guide to all interested in Selecting or Building a House, with full Estimates of Cost, Quantities, &c. By C. J. RICHARDSON. Third Edition. With nearly 600 Illustrations. Crown 8vo, cloth extra, 7*s.* 6*d.*

*** *This book is intended to supply a long-felt want, viz., a plain, non-technical account of every style of house, with the cost and manner of building; it gives every variety, from a workman's cottage to a nobleman's palace.*

FAIRHOLT.—TOBACCO: Its History and Associations; including an Account of the Plant and its Manufacture; with its Modes of Use in all Ages and Countries. By F. W. FAIRHOLT, F.S.A. With Coloured Frontispiece and upwards of 100 Illustrations by the Author. Crown 8vo, cloth extra, 6*s.* [*In the press.*

FARADAY'S CHEMICAL HISTORY OF A CANDLE. Lectures delivered to a Juvenile Audience. A New Edition, Edited by W. CROOKES, Esq., F.C.S., &c. Crown 8vo, cloth extra, with numerous Illustrations, 4*s.* 6*d.*

FARADAY'S VARIOUS FORCES OF NATURE. A New Edition, Edited by W. CROOKES, Esq., F.C.S., &c. Crown 8vo, cloth extra, with numerous Illustrations, 4*s.* 6*d.*

FIGUIER'S PRIMITIVE MAN: A Popular Manual of the prevailing Theories of the Descent of Man as promulgated by DARWIN, LYELL, Sir JOHN LUBBOCK, HUXLEY, E. B. TYLOR, and other eminent Ethnologists. Translated from the last French edition, and revised by E. B. T. With 263 Illustrations. Demy 8vo, cloth extra, gilt, 9*s.*

"An interesting and essentially popular resumé of all that has been written on the subject. M. Figuier has collected together the evidences which modern researches have accumulated, and has done this with a considerable amount of care. He endeavours to separate the inquiry respecting Primitive Man from the Mosaic account of Man's creation, and does not admit that the authority of Holy Writ is in any way questioned by those labours which aim at seeking the real epoch of Man's first appearance upon earth. . . . An interesting book, with 263 illustrations, of which thirty are full-page engravings, confessedly somewhat fanciful in their combinations, but which will be found on examination to be justified by that soundest evidence, the actual discovery of the objects of which they represent the use."—*Athenæum.*

FINGER-RING LORE: Historical and Anecdotal. By WILLIAM JONES, F.S.A. With Hundreds of Illustrations of Curious Rings of all Ages and Countries. Crown 8vo, cloth extra, gilt, 7*s.* 6*d.* [*In the press.*

FINISH TO LIFE IN AND OUT OF LONDON; or, The Final Adventures of Tom, Jerry, and Logic. By PIERCE EGAN. Royal 8vo, cloth extra, with spirited Coloured Illustrations by CRUIKSHANK, 21s.

FLAGELLATION AND THE FLAGELLANTS.—A History of the Rod in all Countries, from the Earliest Period to the Present Time. By the Rev. W. COOPER, B.A. Third Edition, revised and corrected, with numerous Illustrations. Thick crown 8vo, cloth extra, gilt, 12s. 6d.

FOX'S BOOK OF MARTYRS: The Acts and Monuments of the Church. Edited by JOHN CUMMING, D.D. With upwards of 1000 Illustrations. Three Vols., imperial 8vo, cloth extra, £2 12s. 6d.

GELL'S TOPOGRAPHY OF ROME AND ITS VICINITY. A New Edition, revised and enlarged by E. H. BUNBURY. With a large mounted Map of Rome and its Environs (from a careful Trigonometrical Survey). Two Vols., 8vo, cloth extra, 15s.

GELL AND GANDY'S POMPEIANA; or, The Topography, Edifices, and Ornaments of Pompeii. With upwards of 100 Line Engravings by GOODALL, COOKE, HEATH, PYE, &c. Demy 8vo, cloth extra, gilt, 18s.

GEMMER'S (Mrs.) PLEASANT RHYMES FOR LITTLE READERS. By CAROLINE M. GEMMER (GERDA FAY). With numerous Illustrations. Crown 8vo, cloth extra. [*In the press.*

GEMS OF ART: A Collection of 36 Engravings, after Paintings by REMBRANDT, CUYP, REYNOLDS, POUSSIN, MURILLO, TENIERS, CORREGGIO, GAINSBOROUGH, NORTHCOTE, &c., executed in Mezzotint by TURNER, BROMLEY, &c. Folio, in Portfolio, £1 11s. 6d.

GENIAL SHOWMAN; or, Show Life in the New World. Adventures with Artemus Ward, and the Story of his Life. By E. P. HINGSTON. Third Edition. Crown 8vo, Illustrated by W. BRUNTON, cloth extra, 7s. 6d.

GIBBON'S ROMAN EMPIRE (The Decline and Fall of the). With Memoir of the Author, and full General Index. Imperial 8vo, with Portrait, cloth extra, 15s.

GILBERT'S (W. S.) DRAMATIC WORKS ("A Wicked World," "Charity," "Palace of Truth," "Pygmalion," "Trial by Jury," &c.). One Vol., crown 8vo, cloth extra. [*In the press.*

GIL BLAS.—HISTORIA DE GIL BLAS DE SANTILLANA. Por LE SAGE. Traducida al Castellano por el PADRE ISLA. Nueva Edicion, corregida y revisada. Complete in One Vol., post 8vo, cl. extra, nearly 600 pp., 4s. 6d.

GILLRAY'S CARICATURES. Printed from the Original Plates, all engraved by Himself between 1779 and 1810; comprising the best Political and Humorous Satires of the Reign of GEORGE THE THIRD, in upwards of 600 highly spirited Engravings. Atlas folio, half-morocco extra, gilt edges, £7 10s.—There is also a Volume of the SUPPRESSED PLATES, atlas folio, half-morocco, 31s. 6d.—Also, a VOLUME OF LETTERPRESS DESCRIPTIONS, comprising a very amusing Political History of the Reign of GEORGE THE THIRD, by THOS. WRIGHT and R. H. EVANS. Demy 8vo, cloth extra, 15s.; or half-morocco, £1 1s.

GILLRAY, THE CARICATURIST: The Story of his Life and Times, and Anecdotal Descriptions of his Engravings. Edited by THOMAS WRIGHT, Esq., M.A., F.S.A. With 83 full-page Plates, and numerous Wood Engravings. Demy 4to, 600 pages, cloth extra, 31s. 6d.

"High as the expectations excited by this description [in the Introduction] may be, they will not be disappointed. The most inquisitive or exacting reader will find ready gathered to his hand, without the trouble of reference, almost every scrap of narrative, anecdote, gossip, scandal, or epigram, in poetry or prose, that he can possibly require for the elucidation of the caricatures."—*Quarterly Review.*

GLEIG'S CHELSEA PENSIONERS: Saratoga, the Rivals, and other Stories. By the Rev. G. R. GLEIG, late Chaplain to Her Majesty's Forces. Post 8vo, illustrated boards, 2*s.*

GOLDEN LIBRARY.

Square 16mo (Tauchnitz size), cloth, extra gilt, price 2*s.* per Vol.

BYRON'S DON JUAN.

CLERICAL ANECDOTES: Humours of "the Cloth."

HOLMES'S AUTOCRAT OF THE BREAKFAST TABLE. With an Introduction by GEORGE AUGUSTUS SALA.

HOLMES'S PROFESSOR AT THE BREAKFAST TABLE.

HOOD'S WHIMS AND ODDITIES. Both Series Complete in One Volume, with all the original Illustrations.

IRVING'S (Washington) TALES OF A TRAVELLER.

IRVING'S (Washington) TALES OF THE ALHAMBRA.

JESSE'S (Edward) SCENES AND OCCUPATIONS OF COUNTRY LIFE; with Recollections of Natural History.

LAMB'S ESSAYS OF ELIA. Both Series Complete in One Vol.

LEIGH HUNT'S ESSAYS: A Tale for a Chimney Corner, and other Pieces. With Portrait, and Introduction by EDMUND OLLIER.

MALLORY'S (Sir Thomas) MORT D'ARTHUR: The Stories of King Arthur and of the Knights of the Round Table. Edited by B. M. RANKING.

PASCAL'S PROVINCIAL LETTERS. A New Translation, with Historical Introduction and Notes, by T. M'CRIE, D.D., LL.D.

POPE'S COMPLETE POETICAL WORKS. Reprinted from the Original Editions.

ROCHEFOUCAULD'S MAXIMS AND MORAL REFLECTIONS. With Notes, and an Introductory Essay by SAINTE-BEUVE.

ST. PIERRE'S PAUL AND VIRGINIA AND THE INDIAN COTTAGE. Edited, with Life, by the Rev. E. CLARKE.

SHELLEY'S EARLY POEMS, AND QUEEN MAB, with Essay by LEIGH HUNT.

SHELLEY'S LATER POEMS: Laon and Cythna, &c.

SHELLEY'S POSTHUMOUS POEMS, the SHELLEY PAPERS, &c.

SHELLEY'S PROSE WORKS, including A Refutation of Deism, Zastrozzi, St. Irvyne, &c.

WHITE'S NATURAL HISTORY OF SELBORNE. Edited, with additions, by THOMAS BROWN, F.L.S.

GOLDEN TREASURY OF THOUGHT. An Encyclopædia of Quotations from Writers of all Times and all Countries. Selected and Edited by THEODORE TAYLOR. Crown 8vo, cloth gilt, and gilt edges, 7*s.* 6*d.*

GOSPELS (The Holy). Illustrated with upwards of 200 Wood Engravings, after the best Masters, and every page surrounded by ornamental Borders. Handsomely printed, imperial 4to, cloth, full gilt (Grolier style), 10*s.* 6*d.*

GRAMMONT (Count), MEMOIRS OF. By ANTHONY HAMILTON. A New Edition, with a Biographical Sketch of Count Hamilton, numerous Historical and Illustrative Notes by Sir WALTER SCOTT, and 64 Copperplate Portraits by EDWARD SCRIVEN. 8vo, cloth extra, 12*s.* 6*d.* [*In the press.*

GREENWOOD'S (James) LOW-LIFE DEEPS: An Account of Strange Fish to be found there; including "The Man and Dog Fight," with much additional and confirmatory evidence; "With a Tally-Man," "A Fallen Star," "The Betting Barber," "A Coal Marriage," &c. With Illustrations in tint by ALFRED CONCANEN. Crown 8vo, cloth extra, gilt, 7s. 6d. [*In the press.*

GREENWOOD'S WILDS OF LONDON; Descriptive Sketches from Personal Observations and Experience of Remarkable Scenes, People, and Places in London. By JAMES GREENWOOD, the "Lambeth Casual." With 12 Tinted Illustrations by ALFRED CONCANEN. Crown 8vo, cloth extra, gilt, 7s. 6d.

"Mr. James Greenwood presents himself once more in the character of 'one whose delight it is to do his humble endeavour towards exposing and extirpating social abuses and those hole-and-corner evils which afflict society.'"—*Saturday Review.*

GREVILLE'S CRYPTOGAMIC FLORA. Comprising the Principal Species found in Great Britain, inclusive of all the New Species recently discovered in Scotland. Six Vols., royal 8vo, with 360 beautifully Coloured Plates, half-morocco, gilt, £7 7s.; the Plates uncoloured, £4 14s. 6d.

"A truly admirable work, which may be honestly designated as so excellent, that nothing can be found to compete with it in the whole range of Indigenous Botany; whether we consider the importance of its critical discussions, the accuracy of the drawings, the minuteness of the analyses, or the unusual care which is evident in the publishing department."—LOUDON.

GRIMM.—GERMAN POPULAR STORIES. Collected by the Brothers GRIMM, and Translated by EDGAR TAYLOR. Edited, with an Introduction, by JOHN RUSKIN. With 22 Illustrations after the inimitable designs of GEORGE CRUIKSHANK. Both Series Complete. Square crown 8vo, 6s. 6d.; gilt leaves, 7s. 6d.

"The illustrations of this volume . . . . are of quite sterling and admirable art, of a class precisely parallel in elevation to the character of the tales which they illustrate; and the original etchings, as I have before said in the Appendix to my 'Elements of Drawing,' were unrivalled in masterfulness of touch since Rembrandt (in some qualities of delineation, unrivalled even by him). . . . . To make somewhat enlarged copies of them, looking at them through a magnifying glass, and never putting two lines where Cruikshank has put only one, would be an exercise in decision and severe drawing which would leave afterwards little to be learnt in schools."—*Extract from Introduction by* JOHN RUSKIN.

GUYOT'S EARTH AND MAN; or, Physical Geography in its Relation to the History of Mankind. With Additions by Professors AGASSIZ, PIERCE, and GRAY. With 12 Maps and Engravings on Steel, some Coloured, and a copious Index. A New Edition. Crown 8vo, cloth extra, gilt, 4s. 6d.

HAKE'S (T. GORDON) NEW SYMBOLS: Poems. By the Author of "Parables and Tales." Crown 8vo, cloth extra. [*In the press.*

HALL'S (Mrs. S. C.) SKETCHES OF IRISH CHARACTER. With numerous Illustrations on Steel and Wood, by DANIEL MACLISE, Sir JOHN GILBERT, W. HARVEY, and G. CRUIKSHANK. 8vo, cloth extra, gilt, 7s. 6d.

"The Irish sketches of this lady resemble Miss Mitford's beautiful English Sketches in 'Our Village,' but they are far more vigorous and picturesque and bright."—*Blackwood's Magazine.*

HALL-MARKS (BOOK OF); or, Manual of Reference for the Goldsmith and Silversmith. By ALFRED LUTSCHAUNIG. Crown 8vo, with 46 Plates of the Hall-marks of the different Assay Towns of the Kingdom. 7s. 6d.

HARRIS'S AURELIAN; A Natural History of English Moths and Butterflies, and the Plants on which they feed. A New Edition. Edited, with Additions, by J. O. WESTWOOD. With about 400 exquisitely Coloured Figures of Moths, Butterflies, Caterpillars, &c., and the Plants on which they feed. Small folio, half-morocco extra, gilt edges, £3 13s. 6d

HAYDON'S (B. R.) MEMOIR, CORRESPONDENCE, AND TABLE-TALK. By his Son, F. W. HAYDON. Comprising a large number of hitherto unpublished Letters from KEATS, WILKIE, SOUTHEY, WORDSWORTH, KIRKUP, LAMB, LEIGH HUNT, LANDSEER, and others. Two Volumes, demy 8vo, cloth extra, illustrated with a Portrait and facsimiles of many interesting Sketches; including a Portrait of HAYDON drawn by KEATS, and HAYDON'S Portraits of WILKIE, KEATS, LEIGH HUNT, and MARIA FOOTE, Sketched by him in his Journals. [*In the press.*

HEEREN'S HISTORICAL WORKS. Translated from the German by GEORGE BANCROFT, and various Oxford Scholars. Six Vols., 8vo, cloth extra, £1 16*s.*; or, separately, 6*s.* per volume.

*** *The Contents of the Volumes are as follows:*—Vols. 1 and 2. Historical Researches into the Politics, Intercourse, and Trade of the Ancient Nations of Asia; 3. Researches into the Politics, Intercourse, and Trade of the Ancient Nations of Africa, including the Carthaginians, Ethiopians, and Egyptians; 4. History of the Political System of Europe and its Colonies; 5. History of Ancient Greece, with Historical Treatises; 6. A Manual of Ancient History, with special reference to the Constitutions, Commerce, and Colonies of the States of Antiquity.

"Prof. Heeren's Historical Researches stand in the very highest rank among those with which modern Germany has enriched European literature."—*Quarterly Review.*

"We look upon Heeren as having breathed a new life into the dry bones of Ancient History. In countries, the history of which has been too imperfectly known to afford lessons of political wisdom, he has taught us still more interesting lessons—on the social relations of men, and the intercourse of nations in the earlier ages of the world. His work is as learned as a professed commentary on the ancient historians and geographers, and as entertaining as a modern book of travels."—*Edinburgh Review.*

HISTORICAL PORTRAITS; Upwards of 430 Engravings of Rare Prints. Comprising the Collections of RODD and GRAINGER, RICHARDSON, CAULFIELD, &c. With Descriptive Text to every Plate, giving a brief outline of the most important Historical and Biographical Facts and Dates connected with each Portrait, and references to original Authorities. In Three Vols., royal 4to, Roxburghe binding, price £6 6*s.* [*In the press.*

THE ORIGINAL HOGARTH.

HOGARTH'S WORKS. ENGRAVED BY HIMSELF. 153 fine Plates, with elaborate Letterpress Descriptions by JOHN NICHOLS. Atlas folio, half-morocco extra, gilt edges, £7 10*s.*

"I was pleased with the reply of a gentleman who, being asked which book he esteemed most in his library, answered 'Shakespeare'; being asked which he esteemed next best, answered 'Hogarth.'"—CHARLES LAMB.

HOGARTH'S WORKS. With Life and Anecdotal Descriptions of the Pictures, by JOHN IRELAND and JOHN NICHOLS. 160 Engravings, reduced in exact facsimile of the Originals. The whole in Three Series, 8vo, cloth, gilt, 22*s.* 6*d.*; or, separately, 7*s.* 6*d.* per volume.

HOGARTH'S WORKS. Engraved by T. COOK. 84 Plates, atlas folio, half-morocco, £5.

HOGARTH MORALIZED: A Complete Edition of all the most capital and admired Works of WILLIAM HOGARTH, accompanied by concise and comprehensive Explanations of their Moral Tendency, by the late Rev. Dr. TRUSLER; to which are added, an Introductory Essay, and many Original and Selected Notes, by JOHN MAJOR. With 57 Plates and numerous Woodcuts. New Edition, revised, corrected, and enlarged. Demy 8vo, hf.-Roxburghe, 12*s.* 6*d.*

HOGARTH'S FIVE DAYS' FROLIC; or, Peregrinations by Land and Water. Illustrated by Tinted Drawings, made by HOGARTH and SCOTT during the Journey. Demy 4to, cloth extra, gilt, 10*s.* 6*d.*

HOLBEIN'S PORTRAITS OF THE COURT OF HENRY THE EIGHTH. A Series of 84 exquisitely beautiful Tinted Plates, engraved by BARTOLOZZI, COOPER, and others, and printed on Tinted Paper, in imitation of the Original Drawings in the Royal Collection at Windsor. With Historical Letterpress by EDMUND LODGE, Norroy King of Arms. Imperial 4to, half-morocco extra, gilt edges, £5 15*s*. 6*d*.

HOLBEIN'S PORTRAITS OF THE COURT OF HENRY VIII. CHAMBERLAINE'S Imitations of the Original Drawings, mostly engraved by BARTOLOZZI. London: printed by W. BULMER & Co., Shakespeare Printing Office, 1792. 92 splendid Portraits (including 8 additional Plates), elaborately tinted in Colours, with Descriptive and Biographical Notes, by EDMUND LODGE, Norroy King of Arms. Atlas fol., half-morocco, gilt edges, £20.—The same, PROOF IMPRESSIONS, uncoloured, half-Roxburghe, £18.

HONE'S SCRAP-BOOKS: The Miscellaneous Collections of WILLIAM HONE, Author of "The Table-Book," "Every-Day Book," and "Year-Book": being a Supplementary Volume to those works. Now first published. With Notes, Portraits, and numerous Illustrations of curious and eccentric objects. Crown 8vo. [*In preparation.*

HOOD'S (Thomas) CHOICE WORKS, in Prose and Verse. Including the Cream of the Comic Annuals. With Life of the Author, Portrait, and over Two Hundred original Illustrations. Crown 8vo, cloth extra, gilt, 7*s*. 6*d*. [*In the press.*

HOOD'S (Tom) FROM NOWHERE TO THE NORTH POLE: A Noah's Arkæological Narrative. By TOM HOOD. With 25 Illustrations by W. BRUNTON and E. C. BARNES. Square crown 8vo, in a handsome and specially-designed binding, gilt edges, 6*s*.

"Poor Tom Hood! It is very sad to turn over the droll pages of 'From Nowhere to the North Pole,' and to think that he will never make the young people, for whom, like his famous father, he ever had such a kind, sympathetic heart, laugh or cry any more. This is a birthday story, and no part of it is better than the first chapter, concerning birthdays in general, and Frank's birthday in particular. The amusing letterpress is profusely interspersed with the jingling rhymes which children love and learn so easily. Messrs. Brunton and Barnes do full justice to the writer's meaning, and a pleasanter result of the harmonious co-operation of author and artist could not be desired."—*Times.*

HOOD'S (Tom) HUMOROUS WORKS. Edited, with an Introduction, by his Sister, FRANCES FREELING BRODERIP. Crown 8vo, cloth extra, and numerous Illustrations, 6*s*. [*In the press.*

HOOKER'S (Sir William) EXOTIC FLORA. Containing Figures and Descriptions of Rare or otherwise interesting Exotic Plants. With Remarks upon their Generic and Specific Characters, Natural Orders, Culture, &c. Containing 232 large and beautifully Coloured Plates. Three Vols., imperial 8vo, cloth extra, gilt, £6 6*s*.

HOOKER AND GREVILLE'S ICONES FILICUM; or, Figures and Descriptions of Ferns, many of which have been altogether unnoticed by Botanists, or have been incorrectly figured. With 240 beautifully Coloured Plates. Two Vols., folio, half-morocco, gilt, £12 12*s*.

HOPE'S COSTUME OF THE ANCIENTS. Illustrated in upwards of 320 Outline Engravings, containing Representations of Egyptian, Greek, and Roman Habits and Dresses. A New Edition. Two Vols., royal 8vo, with Coloured Frontispieces, cloth extra, £2 5*s*.

HORNE.—ORION. An Epic Poem, in Three Books. By RICHARD HENGIST HORNE. With Photographic Portrait. TENTH EDITION. Crown 8vo, cloth extra, 7*s*.

"Orion will be admitted, by every man of genius, to be one of the noblest, if not the very noblest poetical work of the age. Its defects are trivial and conventional, its beauties intrinsic and supreme."—EDGAR ALLAN POE.

HUME AND SMOLLETT'S HISTORY OF ENGLAND. With a Memoir of HUME by himself, Chronological Table of Contents, and General Index. Imperial 8vo, with Portraits of the Authors, cloth extra, 15*s.*

HUNT'S (Robert) DROLL STORIES OF OLD CORNWALL; or, POPULAR ROMANCES OF THE WEST OF ENGLAND. With Illustrations by GEORGE CRUIKSHANK. Crown 8vo, cloth extra, gilt, 7*s.* 6*d.*

ITALIAN MASTERS (DRAWINGS BY THE): Autotype Facsimiles of Original Drawings. With Critical and Descriptive Notes by J. COMYNS CARR. Atlas folio, half-morocco, gilt. [*In preparation.*

ITALIAN SCHOOL OF DESIGN (The): 91 beautiful Plates, chiefly Engraved by BARTOLOZZI, after Paintings in the Royal Collection by MICHAEL ANGELO, DOMENICHINO, ANNIBALE CARACCI, and others. Imperial 4to, half-morocco, gilt edges, £2 12*s.* 6*d.*

JARDINE'S (Sir Wm.) NATURALIST'S LIBRARY. 42 vols. Fcap. 8vo, illustrated by over 1200 Coloured Plates, with numerous Portrait and Memoirs of eminent Naturalists, half (imitation) calf, full gilt, top edges gilt, £9 9*s.*; or, separately, cloth extra, 4*s.* 6*d.* per Vol., as follows:—

Vols. 1 to 4. British Birds; 5. Sun Birds: 6 and 7. Humming Birds; 8. Game Birds; 9. Pigeons; 10. Parrots; 11 and 12. Birds of West Africa; 13. Fly Catchers; 14. Pheasants, Peacocks, &c.; 15. Animals—Introduction; 16. Lions and Tigers; 17. British Quadrupeds; 18 and 19. Dogs; 20. Horses; 21 and 22. Ruminating Animals; 23. Elephants, &c.; 24. Marsupialia; 25. Seals, &c.; 26. Whales, &c.; 27. Monkeys; 28. Insects—Introduction; 29. British Butterflies; 30. British Moths, &c.; 31. Foreign Butterflies; 32. Foreign Moths; 33. Beetles; 34. Bees; 35. Fishes—Introduction, and Foreign Fishes; 36 and 37. British Fishes; 38. Perch, &c.; 39 and 40. Fishes of Guiana; 41. Smith's Natural History of Man; 42. Gould's Humming Birds.

JENNINGS' (Hargrave) ONE OF THE THIRTY. With numerous curious Illustrations. Crown 8vo, cloth extra, 10*s.* 6*d.*

JENNINGS' (Hargrave) THE ROSICRUCIANS: Their Rites and Mysteries. With Chapters on the Ancient Fire and Serpent Worshippers, and Explanations of Mystic Symbols in Monuments and Talismans of Primeval Philosophers. Crown 8vo, with 300 Illustrations, 10*s.* 6*d.*

JERROLD'S (Douglas) THE BARBER'S CHAIR, AND THE HEDGEHOG LETTERS. Edited, with an Introduction, by his Son, BLANCHARD JERROLD. Crown 8vo, with Steel-plate Portrait, cloth extra, 7*s.* 6*d.*

"Better fitted than any other of his productions to give an idea of Douglas Jerrold's amazing wit; the 'Barber's Chair' may be presumed to give as near an approach as is possible in print to the wit of Jerrold's conversation."—*Examiner.*

JOHNSON'S ENGLISH DICTIONARY. Printed verbatim from the Author's Last and most Complete Edition, with all the Examples in full; to which are prefixed a History of the Language and a Grammar of the English Tongue. Imperial 8vo, cloth extra, 15*s.*

JOHNSON'S LIVES OF ENGLISH HIGHWAYMEN, PIRATES, AND ROBBERS. With Additions by WHITEHEAD. Fcap. 8vo, 16 Plates, cloth extra, gilt, 5*s.*

JOSEPHUS (The Works of). Translated by WHISTON. Containing both the "Antiquities of the Jews," and the "Wars of the Jews." Two Vols., 8vo, with 52 Illustrations and Maps, cloth extra, gilt, 14*s.*

KINGSLEY'S (Henry) NUMBER SEVENTEEN: A Novel. In Two Vols., crown 8vo, cloth extra, price 21*s.*, at all Libraries.

KNIGHT'S (H. Gally) ECCLESIASTICAL ARCHITECTURE OF ITALY, from the time of Constantine to the Fifteenth Century, with Introduction and descriptive Text. Complete in Two Series; the FIRST, to the end of the Eleventh Century; the SECOND, from the Twelfth to the Fifteenth Century: containing 81 beautiful Views of Ecclesiastical Buildings in Italy, several of them Illuminated in gold and colours Imperial folio, half-morocco extra, price £3 13s. 6d. each Series.

LAMB'S (Charles) COMPLETE WORKS, in Prose and Verse, reprinted from the Original Editions, with many pieces now first included in any Edition, and Notes and Introduction by R. H. SHEPHERD. With Two Portraits and facsimile of a page of the "Essay on Roast Pig." Crown 8vo, cloth extra, gilt, 7s. 6d.

"A complete edition of Lamb's writings, in prose and verse, has long been wanted, and is now supplied. The editor appears to have taken great pains to bring together Lamb's scattered contributions, and his collection contains a number of pieces which are now reproduced for the first time since their original appearance in various old periodicals."—*Saturday Review.*

LAMB (Mary and Charles): THEIR POEMS, LETTERS, and REMAINS. With Reminiscences and Notes by W. CAREW HAZLITT. With HANCOCK'S Portrait of the Essayist, Facsimiles of the Title-pages of the rare First Editions of Lamb's and Coleridge's Works, and numerous Illustrations. Crown 8vo, cloth extra, 10s. 6d.; Large Paper copies, 21s.

"Must be consulted by all future biographers of the Lambs."—*Daily News.*

"Very many passages will delight those fond of literary trifles; hardly any portion will fail in interest for lovers of Charles Lamb and his sister."—*Standard.*

LAMONT'S YACHTING IN THE ARCTIC SEAS: An Examination of Routes to the North Pole, during Five Voyages of Sport and Discovery in the Neighbourhood of the Great Ice Pack. By JAMES LAMONT, F.G.S., F.R.G.S., Author of "Seasons with the Sea-Horses." Edited, with numerous full-page Illustrations, by WILLIAM LIVESAY, M.D. Demy 8vo, cloth extra, with Maps and Illustrations. [*In the press.*

LANDSEER'S (Sir Edwin) ETCHINGS OF CARNIVOROUS ANIMALS. Comprising 38 subjects, chiefly Early Works, etched by his Brother THOMAS or his Father, with Letterpress Descriptions. Roy. 4to, cloth extra 15s.

LEE (General Robert): HIS LIFE AND CAMPAIGNS. By his Nephew, EDWARD LEE CHILDE. With Steel-plate Portrait by JEENS, and a Map. Post 8vo, 9s.

LIFE IN LONDON; or, The Day and Night Scenes of Jerry Hawthorn and Corinthian Tom. WITH THE WHOLE OF CRUIKSHANK'S VERY DROLL ILLUSTRATIONS, in Colours, after the Originals. Cr. 8vo, cloth extra, 7s. 6d.

LINTON'S (Mrs. E. Lynn) PATRICIA KEMBALL: A Novel. New and Popular Edition, with a Frontispiece by GEORGE DU MAURIER. Crown 8vo, cloth extra, gilt, 6s.

"A very clever and well-constructed story, original and striking, and interesting all through. . . . A novel abounding in thought and power and interest."—*Times.*

"Perhaps the ablest novel published in London this year (1874) . . . We know of nothing in the novels we have lately read equal to the scene in which Mr. Hamley proposes to Dora . . . We advise our readers to send to the library for the story." —*Athenæum.*

"This novel is distinguished by qualities which entitle it to a place apart from the ordinary fiction of the day; . . . displays genuine humour, as well as keen social observation. . . . . Enough graphic portraiture and witty observation to furnish materials for half a dozen novels of the ordinary kind."—*Saturday Review.*

LINTON'S (Mrs. E. Lynn) JOSHUA DAVIDSON, CHRISTIAN AND COMMUNIST. SIXTH EDITION, with a New Preface. Small crown 8vo, cloth extra, 4s. 6d.

LONDON.—WILKINSON'S LONDINA ILLUSTRATA; or, Graphic and Historical Illustrations of the most Interesting and Curious Architectural Monuments of the City and Suburbs of London and Westminster (now mostly destroyed). Two Vols., imperial 4to, containing 207 Copperplate Engravings, with historical and descriptive Letterpress, half-bound morocco, top edges gilt, £5 5s.

*** *An enumeration of a few of the Plates will give some idea of the scope of the Work*:—St. Bartholomew's Church, Cloisters, and Priory, in 1393: St. Michael's, Cornhill, in 1421; St. Paul's Cathedral and Cross, in 1616 and 1656; St. John's of Jerusalem, Clerkenwell, 1660; Bunyan's Meeting House, in 1687; Guildhall, in 1517; Cheapside and its Cross, in 1547, 1585, and 1641; Cornhill, in 1599; Merchant Taylors' Hall, in 1599; Shakespeare's Globe Theatre, in 1612 and 1647; Alleyne's Bear Garden, in 1614 and 1647; Drury Lane, in 1792 and 1814; Covent Garden, in 1732, 1794, and 1809; Whitehall, in 1638 and 1697; York House, with Inigo Jones's Water Gate, circa 1626; Somerset House, previous to its alteration by Inigo Jones, circa 1600: St James's Palace, 1660; Montagu House (now the British Museum) before 1685, and in 1804.

LONGFELLOW'S PROSE WORKS, Complete. With Portrait and Illustrations by VALENTINE BROMLEY. 800 pages, crown 8vo, cloth gilt, 7s. 6d.

*** *This is by far the most complete edition ever issued in this country. "Outre-Mer" contains two additional chapters, restored from the first edition; while "The Poets and Poetry of Europe," and the little collection of Sketches entitled "Driftwood," are now first introduced to the English public.*

LONGFELLOW'S POETICAL WORKS. With numerous fine Illustrations. Crown 8vo, cloth extra, gilt, 7s. 6d. [*In the press.*

LOST BEAUTIES OF THE ENGLISH LANGUAGE. An Appeal to Authors, Poets, Clergymen, and Public Speakers. By CHARLES MACKAY, LL.D. Crown 8vo, cloth extra, 6s. 6d.

LOTOS LEAVES: Original Stories, Essays, and Poems, by WILKIE COLLINS, MARK TWAIN, WHITELAW REID, JOHN HAY, NOAH BROOKS, JOHN BROUGHAM, P. V. NASBY, ISAAC BROMLEY, and others. Profusely Illustrated by ALFRED FREDERICKS, ARTHUR LUMLEY, JOHN LA FARGE, GILBERT BURLING, GEORGE WHITE, and others. Crown 4to, handsomely bound, cloth extra, gilt and gil edges, 21s.

"A very comely and pleasant volume, produced by general contribution of a literary club in New York, which has some kindly relations with a similar coterie in London. A *livre de luxe*, splendidly illustrated."—*Daily Telegraph.*

MACLISE'S GALLERY OF ILLUSTRIOUS LITERARY CHARACTERS. (THE FAMOUS FRASER PORTRAITS.) With Notes by the late WILLIAM MAGINN, LL.D. Edited, with copious Additional Notes, by WILLIAM BATES, B.A. The volume contains 83 CHARACTERISTIC PORTRAITS, now first issued in a complete form. Demy 4to, cloth gilt and gilt edges, 31s. 6d.

"One of the most interesting volumes of this year's literature."—*Times.*

"Deserves a place on every drawing-room table, and may not unfitly be removed from the drawing-room to the library."—*Spectator.*

MACQUOID'S (Katharine S., Author of "Patty," &c.) THE EVIL EYE, and other Stories. With 8 Illustrations by THOMAS R. MACQUOID and PERCY MACQUOID. Crown 8vo, cloth extra, price 6s. [*In the press.*

MADRE NATURA versus THE MOLOCH OF FASHION. By LUKE LIMNER. With 32 Illustrations by the Author. FOURTH EDITION, revised and enlarged. Crown 8vo, cloth, extra gilt, 2s. 6d.

"Agreeably written and amusingly illustrated. Common sense and erudition are brought to bear on the subjects discussed in it."—*Lancet.*

MAGNA CHARTA. An exact Facsimile of the Original Document in the British Museum, printed on fine plate paper, nearly 3 feet long by 2 feet wide, with the Arms and Seals of the Barons emblazoned in Gold and Colours. Price 5*s*.

A full Translation, with Notes, printed on a large sheet, price 6*d*.

MANTELL'S PICTORIAL ATLAS OF FOSSIL REMAINS. With Additions and Descriptions. 4to, 74 Coloured Plates, cloth extra, 31*s*. 6*d*.

AUTHOR'S CORRECTED EDITION.

MARK TWAIN'S CHOICE WORKS. Revised and Corrected throughout by the Author. With Life, Portrait, and numerous Illustrations. 700 pages, cloth extra, gil 7*s*. 6*d*.

MARK TWAIN'S PLEASURE TRIP on the CONTINENT of EUROPE. Post 8vo, illustrated boards, 2*s*:

MARRYAT'S (Florence) OPEN! SESAME! Three Vols., crown 8vo, 31*s*. 6*d*.

"A story which arouses and sustains the reader's interest to a higher degree than, perhaps, any of its author's former works. . . . A very excellent story."—*Graphic*.

MARSTON'S (Dr. Westland) DRAMATIC and POETICAL WORKS. Collected Library Edition, in Two Vols., crown 8vo. [*In the press.*

MARSTON'S (Philip Bourke) SONG TIDE, and other Poems. Second Edition. Crown 8vo, cloth extra, 8*s*.

"This is a first work of extraordinary performance and of still more extraordinary promise. The youngest school of English poetry has received an important accession to its ranks in Philip Bourke Marston."—*Examiner*.

MARSTON'S (P. B.) ALL IN ALL: Poems and Sonnets. Crown 8vo, cloth extra, 8*s*.

"Many of these poems are leavened with the leaven of genuine poetical sentiment, and expressed with grace and beauty of language. A tender melancholy, as well as a penetrating pathos, gives character to much of their sentiment, and lends it an irresistible interest to all who can feel."—*Standard*.

MAXWELL'S LIFE OF THE DUKE OF WELLINGTON. Three Vols., 8vo, with numerous highly finished Line and Wood Engravings by Eminent Artists. Cloth extra, gilt, £1 7*s*.

MAYHEW'S LONDON CHARACTERS: Illustrations of the Humour, Pathos, and Peculiarities of London Life. By HENRY MAYHEW, Author of "London Labour and the London Poor," and other Writers. With nearly 100 graphic Illustrations by W. S. GILBERT and others. Crown 8vo, cloth extra, 6*s*.

"Well fulfils the promise of its title. . . The book is an eminently interesting one, and will probably attract many readers."—*Court Circular*.

MILLINGEN'S ANCIENT UNEDITED MONUMENTS; comprising Painted Greek Vases, Statues, Busts, Bas-Reliefs, and other Remains of Grecian Art. 62 beautiful Engravings, mostly Coloured, with Letterpress Descriptions. Imperial 4to, half-morocco, £4 14*s*. 6*d*.

MEYRICK'S ENGRAVED ILLUSTRATIONS OF ANCIENT ARMS AND ARMOUR. 154 highly finished Etchings of the Collection at Goodrich Court, Herefordshire, engraved by JOSEPH SKELTON, with Historical and Critical Disquisitions by Sir S. R. MEYRICK. Two Vols., imperial 4to, with Portrait, half-morocco extra, gilt edges, £4 14*s*. 6*d*.

MEYRICK'S PAINTED ILLUSTRATIONS OF ANCIENT ARMS AND ARMOUR: A Critical Inquiry into Ancient Armour as it existed in Europe, but particularly in England, from the Norman Conquest to the Reign of Charles II.; with a Glossary, by Sir S. R. MEYRICK. New and greatly improved Edition, corrected throughout by the Author, with the assistance of ALBERT WAY and others. Illustrated by more than 100 Plates, splendidly Illuminated in gold and silver; also an additional Plate of the Tournament of Locks and Keys. Three Vols., imperial 4to, half-morocco extra, gilt edges, £10 10s.

"While the splendour of the decorations of this work is well calculated to excite curiosity, the novel character of its contents, the very curious extracts from the rare MSS. in which it abounds, and the pleasing manner in which the author's antiquarian researches are prosecuted, will tempt many who take up the book in idleness, to peruse it with care. No previous work can be compared, in point of extent, arrangement, science, or utility, with the one now in question. 1st. It for the first time supplies to our schools of art, correct and ascertained data for costume, in its noblest and most important branch—historical painting. 2nd. It affords a simple, clear, and most conclusive elucidation of a great number of passages in our great dramatic poets—ay, and in the works of those of Greece and Rome--against which commentators and scholiasts have been trying their wits for centuries. 3rd. It throws a flood of light upon the manners, usages, and sports of our ancestors, from the time of the Anglo-Saxons down to the reign of Charles the Second. And lastly, it at once removes a vast number of idle traditions and ingenious fables, which one compiler of history, copying from another, has succeeded in transmitting through the lapse of four or five hundred years.

"It is not often the fortune of a painful student of antiquity to conduct his readers through so splendid a succession of scenes and events as those to which Dr. Meyrick here successively introduces us. But he does it with all the ease and gracefulness of an accomplished *cicerone*. We see the haughty nobles and the impetuous knights—we are present at their arming—assist them to their shields—enter the well-appointed lists with them—and partake the hopes and fears, the perils, honours, and successes of the manly tournaments. Then we are presented to the glorious damsels, all superb and lovely, in 'velours and clothe of golde and dayntie devyces, bothe in pearls and emerawds, sawphires and dymondes,'—and the banquet, with the serving men and bucklers, servitors and trenchers—kings and queens—pageants, &c. &c. We feel as if the age of chivalry had returned in all its glory."—*Edinburgh Review.*

MILTON'S COMPLETE WORKS, Prose and Poetical. With an Introductory Essay by ROBERT FLETCHER. Imp. 8vo, with Portraits, cl. extra, 15s.

"It is to be regretted that the prose writings of Milton should, in our time, be so little read. As compositions, they deserve the attention of every man who wishes to become acquainted with the full power of the English language. They abound with passages compared with which the finest declamations of Burke sink into insignificance. They are a perfect field of cloth of gold. The style is stiff with gorgeous embroidery. Not even in the earlier books of the 'Paradise Lost' has the great poet ever risen higher than in those parts of his controversial works in which his feelings, excited by conflict, find a vent in bursts of devotional and lyric rapture. It is, to borrow his own majestic language, 'a sevenfold chorus of hallelujahs and harping symphonies.'"—MACAULAY.

MITFORD'S (Mary Russell) COUNTRY STORIES. With 5 Steel-plate Illustrations. Fcap. 8vo, cloth extra, gilt edges, 3s. 6d.

MONTAGU'S (Lady Mary Wortley) LETTERS AND WORKS. Edited by Lord WHARNCLIFFE. With important Additions and Corrections, derived from the Original Manuscripts, and a New Memoir. Two Vols., 8vo, with fine Steel Portraits, cloth extra, 18s.

"I have heard Dr. Johnson say that he never read but one book through from choice in his whole life, and that book was Lady Mary Wortley Montagu's Letters."—BOSWELL.

MOSES' ANTIQUE VASES, Candelabra, Lamps, Tripods, Pateræ, Tazzas, Tombs, Mausoleums, Sepulchral Chambers, Cinerary Urns, Sarcophagi, Cippi, and other Ornaments. 170 Plates, several of which are coloured; with historical and descriptive Letterpress by THOS. HOPE, F.A.S. Small 4to, cloth extra, 18s.

MONUMENTAL INSCRIPTIONS OF THE WEST INDIES, from the Earliest Date, with Genealogical and Historical Annotations, &c., from Original, Local, and other Sources. Illustrative of the Histories and Genealogies of the Seventeenth Century, the Calendars of State Papers, Peerages, and Baronetages. With Engravings of the Arms of the Principal Families. Chiefly collected on the spot by Capt. J. H. LAWRENCE-ARCHER. Demy 4to, half-Roxburghe, gilt top, 42*s*.

MUSES OF MAYFAIR: Vers de Société of the Nineteenth Century. Including Selections from TENNYSON, BROWNING, SWINBURNE, ROSSETTI, JEAN INGELOW, LOCKER, INGOLDSBY, HOOD, LYTTON, C.S.C., LANDOR, AUSTIN DOBSON, HENRY LEIGH, &c. &c. Edited by H. CHOLMONDELEY-PENNELL. Crown 8vo, cloth extra, gilt, gilt edges, 7*s*. 6*d*.

NAPOLEON III., THE MAN OF HIS TIME. From Caricatures. Part I. THE STORY OF THE LIFE OF NAPOLEON III., as told by J. M. HASWELL. Part II. THE SAME STORY, as told by the POPULAR CARICATURES of the past Thirty-five Years. Crown 8vo, with Coloured Frontispiece and over 100 Caricatures, 7*s* 6*d*.

NATIONAL GALLERY (The). A Selection from its Pictures. By CLAUDE, REMBRANDT, CUYP, Sir DAVID WILKIE, CORREGGIO, GAINSBOROUGH, CANALETTI, VANDYCK, PAUL VERONESE, CARACCI, RUBENS, N. and G. POUSSIN, and other great Masters. Engraved by GEORGE DOO, JOHN BURNETT, WM. FINDEN, JOHN and HENRY LE KEUX, JOHN PYE, WALTER BROMLEY, and others. With descriptive Text. Columbier 4to, cl. extra, full gilt and gilt edges, 42*s*.

NICHOLSON'S FIVE ORDERS of ARCHITECTURE (The Student's Instructor for Drawing and Working the). Demy 8vo, with 41 Plates, cloth extra, 5*s*.

NIEBUHR'S LECTURES ON ROMAN HISTORY, delivered at the University of Bonn Translated into English from the Edition of Dr. M. ISLER, by H. le M. CHEPMELL, M.A., and FRANZ DEMMLER, Ph.D. Three. vols., fcap. 8vo, half (imitation) calf, full gilt back, and top edge gilt, price 13*s*. 6*d*.

OLD BOOKS—FACSIMILE REPRINTS.

ARMY LISTS OF THE ROUNDHEADS AND CAVALIERS IN THE CIVIL WAR, 1642. SECOND EDITION, Corrected and considerably Enlarged. Edited, with Notes and full Index, by EDWARD PEACOCK, F.S.A. 4to, half-Roxburghe, 7*s*. 6*d*.

D'URFEY'S ("Tom") WIT AND MIRTH; or, PILLS TO PURGE MELANCHOLY. Being a Collection of the best Merry Ballads and Songs, Old and New. Fitted to all Humours, having each their proper Tune for either Voice or Instrument; most of the Songs being new set. London: Printed by W. Pearson, for J. Tonson, at Shakespeare's Head, over against Catherine Street in the Strand, 1719. An exact reprint. In Six Vols., large fcap. 8vo, printed on antique laid paper, antique boards, £3 3*s*.

EARLY NEWS SHEET.—The Russian Invasion of Poland in 1563. (Memorabilis et perinde stupenda de crudeli Moscovitarum Expeditione Narratio, e Germanico in Latinum conversa.) An exact Facsimile of a Contemporary Account, with Introduction, Historical Notes, and full Translation. Large fcap. 8vo, antique paper, half-Roxburghe, 7*s*. 6*d*.

ENGLISH ROGUE (The), described in the Life of MERITON LATROON, and other Extravagants, comprehending the most Eminent Cheats of both Sexes. By RICHARD HEAD and FRANCIS KIRKMAN. A Facsimile Reprint of the rare Original Edition (1665–1672), with Frontispiece, Facsimiles of the 12 Copperplates, and Portraits of the Authors. In Four Vols., large fcap. 8vo, printed on antique laid paper, and bound in antique boards, 36*s*.

HOGG'S JACOBITE RELICS OF SCOTLAND: The Songs, Airs, and Legends of the Adherents to the House of Stuart. Collected and Illustrated by JAMES HOGG. Two Vols, demy 8vo. ORIGINAL EDITION. Cloth extra, 28*s*.

OLD BOOKS—continued.

IRELAND FORGERIES.—Confessions of WILLIAM HENRY IRELAND. Containing the Particulars of his Fabrication of the Shakespeare Manuscripts: together with Anecdotes and Opinions (hitherto unpublished) of many Distinguished Persons in the Literary, Political, and Theatrical World. A Facsimile Reprint from the Original Edition, with several additional Facsimiles. Fcap. 8vo, antique paper and boards, 10*s.* 6*d.*; a few Large Paper copies, at 21*s.*

JOE MILLER'S JESTS: The politest Repartees, most elegant Bons-mots, and most pleasing short Stories in the English Language. London: printed by T. Read. 1739. A Facsimile of Orig. Edit. 8vo, half-morocco, 9*s.* 6*d.*

LITTLE LONDON DIRECTORY OF 1677. The Oldest Printed List of the Merchants and Bankers of London. Reprinted from the Rare Original, with Introduction by J. C. HOTTEN. 16mo, binding after the original, 6*s.* 6*d.*

MERRY DROLLERY, Complete; or, a Collection of Jovial Poems, Merry Songs, Witty Drolleries, intermingled with Pleasant Catches. Collected by W.N.C.B.R.S.J.C., Lovers of Wit. The two Parts in 1 Vol. A page-for-page and literal reprint. Edited, with Indexes and Notes, by J. WOODFALL EBSWORTH, M.A. Cantab. Large fcap. 8vo, antique paper and cloth boards, 12*s.* 6*d*: Large paper copies, 25*s.*

MUSARUM DELICIÆ; or, The Muses' Recreation, 1656; Wit Restored, 1658; and Wit's Recreations, 1640. The whole compared with the Originals. With all the Wood Engravings, Plates, Memoirs, and Notes. A New Edition, in Two Vols., large fcap. 8vo, antique paper and boards, 21*s.*

MYSTERY OF THE GOOD OLD CAUSE. Sarcastic Notices of those Members of the Long Parliament that held Places, both Civil and Military, contrary to the Self-denying Ordinance of April 3, 1645; with the Sums of Money and Lands they divided among themselves. Sm. 4to, half-morocco, 7*s.* 6*d.*

RUMP (The); or, An Exact Collection of the Choicest POEMS and SONGS relating to the late Times, and continued by the most eminent Wits; from Anno 1639 to 1661. A Facsimile Reprint of the rare Original Edition (London, 1662), with Frontispiece and Engraved Title-page. In Two Vols., large fcap. 8vo, printed on antique laid paper, and bound in antique boards, 17*s.* 6*d.*

WESTMINSTER DROLLERIES: Being a Choice Collection of Songs and Poems sung at Court and Theatres. With Additions made by a Person of Quality. Now first reprinted in exact Facsimile from the Original Editions of 1671 and 1672. Edited, with an Introduction on the Literature of the Drolleries, a copious Appendix of Notes, Illustrations, and Emendations of Text, Table of Contents, and Index of First Lines, by J. WOODFALL EBSWORTH, M.A., Cantab. Large fcap. 8vo, antique paper and boards, 12*s.* 6*d.*; Large Paper copies, 25*s.*

OLD DRAMATISTS.

BEN JONSON'S WORKS. With Notes, Critical and Explanatory, and a Biographical Memoir by WM. GIFFORD. Edited by Col. CUNNINGHAM. Complete in Three Vols., crown 8vo, cloth extra, gilt, with Portrait, 6*s.* each.

CHAPMAN'S (George) COMPLETE WORKS. Now first Collected. In Three Volumes, crown 8vo, cloth extra, with two Frontispieces, price 18*s.*; or, separately, 6*s.* per vol. Vol. I. contains the Plays complete, including the doubtful ones; Vol. II. the Poems and Minor Translations, with an Introductory Essay by ALGERNON CHARLES SWINBURNE; Vol. III. the Translations of the Iliad and Odyssey.

MARLOWE'S WORKS. Including his Translations. Edited, with Notes and Introduction, by Col. CUNNINGHAM. Crown 8vo, cloth extra, gilt, with Portrait, price 6*s.*

MASSINGER'S PLAYS. From the Text of WM. GIFFORD. With the addition of the Tragedy of "Believe as You List." Edited by Col. CUNNINGHAM. Crown 8vo, cloth extra, gilt, with Portrait, price 6*s.*

OLD SHEKARRY'S FOREST AND FIELD: Life and Adventure in Wild Africa. With 8 Illustrations. Crown 8vo, cloth extra, gilt, 6s.

OLD SHEKARRY'S WRINKLES; or, Hints to Sportsmen and Travellers upon Dress, Equipment, Armament, and Camp Life. A New Edition, with Illustrations. Small crown 8vo, cloth extra, gilt, 6s.

"The book is most comprehensive in its character, nothing necessary to the paraphernalia of the travelling sportsman being omitted, while the hints are given in that plain, unvarnished language which can be easily understood. There are numerous illustrations, and the book has been excellently brought out by the publishers."—*Sportsman.*

ORIGINAL LISTS OF PERSONS OF QUALITY; Emigrants; Religious Exiles; Political Rebels; Serving Men Sold for a Term of Years; Apprentices; Children Stolen; Maidens Pressed; and others who went from Great Britain to the American Plantations, 1600–1700. From MSS. in Her Majesty's Public Record Office. Edited by JOHN CAMDEN HOTTEN. Crown 4to, cloth gilt, 700 pages, 38s. Large Paper copies, half-morocco, 60s.

"This volume is an English Family Record, and as such may be commended to English families, and the descendants of English families, wherever they exist."—*Academy.*

O'SHAUGHNESSY'S (Arthur) AN EPIC OF WOMEN, and other Poems. Second Edition. Fcap. 8vo, cloth extra, 6s.

O'SHAUGHNESSY'S LAYS OF FRANCE. (Founded on the "Lays of Marie.") Second Edition. Crown 8vo, cloth extra, 10s. 6d.

O'SHAUGHNESSY'S MUSIC AND MOONLIGHT: Poems and Songs. Fcap. 8vo, cloth extra, 7s. 6d.

"It is difficult to say which is more exquisite, the technical perfection of structure and melody, or the delicate pathos of thought. Mr. O'Shaughnessy will enrich our literature with some of the very best songs written in our generation."—*Academy.*

OTTLEY'S FACSIMILES OF SCARCE AND CURIOUS PRINTS, by the Early Masters of the Italian, German, and Flemish Schools. 129 Copperplate Engravings, illustrative of the History of Engraving, from the Invention of the Art (the Niellos printed in Silver). Imperial 4to, half-bound morocco, top edges gilt, £6 6s.

OUIDA'S NOVELS.—Uniform Edition, crown 8vo, cloth extra, gilt, price 5s. each.

Folle Farine.

Idalia. A Romance.

Chandos. A Novel.

Under Two Flags.

Cecil Castlemaine's Gage.

Tricotrin. The Story of a Waif and Stray.

Pascarèl. Only a Story.

Held in Bondage; or, Granville de Vigne.

Puck. His Vicissitudes, Adventures, &c.

A Dog of Flanders, and other Stories.

Strathmore; or, Wrought by his Own Hand.

Two Little Wooden Shoes.

"Keen poetic insight, an intense love of nature, a deep admiration of the beautiful in form and colour, are the gifts of Ouida."—*Morning Post.*

PALEY'S COMPLETE WORKS. Containing the Natural Theology, Moral and Political Philosophy, Evidences of Christianity, Horæ Paulinæ, Clergyman's Companion, &c. Demy 8vo, with Portrait, cloth extra, 5s.

PERCY'S RELIQUES OF ANCIENT ENGLISH POETRY. Consisting of Old Heroic Ballads, Songs, and other Pieces of our Earlier Poets, together with some few of later date, and a copious Glossary. Medium 8vo, with Engraved Title and Frontispiece, cloth extra, gilt, 5s.

PARKS OF LONDON: Their History, from the Earliest Period to the Present Time. By JACOB LARWOOD. With numerous Illustrations, Coloured and Plain. Crown 8vo, cloth extra, gilt, 7*s.* 6*d.*

PLATTNER'S MANUAL OF QUALITATIVE AND QUANTITATIVE ANALYSIS WITH THE BLOWPIPE. From the last German Edition. Revised and enlarged by Prof. TH. RICHTER, Royal Saxon Mining Academy. Translated by Prof. H. B. CORNWALL, School of Mines, New York. Edited by T. HUGO COOKESLEY. With numerous Illustrations. Demy 8vo, cloth extra, 21*s.*

"'Plattner's Manual' deservedly stands first among all other works on this subject, and its appearance in English will be hailed by all those who are occupied in the analysis of mineral ores, but who, from ignorance of the German language, have been hitherto unable to study it. It is a work of great practical as well as scientific value."—*Standard.*

"By far the most complete work extant on a subject of growing practical importance and of extreme interest."—*Mining Journal.*

PLUTARCH'S LIVES, Complete. Translated by the LANGHORNES. New Edition, with Medallion Portraits. In Two Vols., 8vo, cloth extra, 10*s.* 6*d.*

POE'S (Edgar Allan) CHOICE PROSE AND POETICAL WORKS. With BAUDELAIRE'S "Essay." 750 pages, crown 8vo, Portrait and Illustrations, cloth extra, 7*s.* 6*d.*

PRACTICAL ASSAYER: A Guide to Miners and Explorers. Giving directions, in the simplest form, for assaying bullion and the baser metals by the cheapest, quickest, and best methods. By OLIVER NORTH. With Tables and Illustrative Woodcuts. Crown 8vo, 7*s.* 6*d.*

PRIVATE BOOK OF USEFUL ALLOYS AND MEMORANDA FOR GOLDSMITHS AND JEWELLERS. By JAMES E. COLLINS, C.E. Royal 16mo, 3*s.* 6*d.*

PROUT, FATHER.—THE FINAL RELIQUES OF FATHER PROUT. Collected and edited, from MSS. supplied by the family of the Rev. FRANCIS MAHONY, by BLANCHARD JERROLD. With Portrait and Facsimiles. [*In the press.*

PUCK ON PEGASUS. By H. CHOLMONDELEY-PENNELL. Profusely illustrated by JOHN LEECH, H. K. BROWNE, Sir NOEL PATON, J. E. MILLAIS, JOHN TENNIEL, RICHARD DOYLE, ELLEN EDWARDS, and other Artists. Seventh Edition, crown 8vo, cloth extra, gilt, price 5*s.*

"The book is clever and amusing, vigorous and healthy."—*Saturday Review.*

PUGIN'S ARCHITECTURAL WORKS.

APOLOGY FOR THE REVIVAL OF CHRISTIAN ARCHITECTURE. With 10 large Etchings. Small 4to, cloth extra, 5*s.*

EXAMPLES OF GOTHIC ARCHITECTURE, selected from Ancient Edifices in England. 225 Engravings by LE KEUX, with descriptive Letterpress by E. J. WILLSON. Three Vols., 4to, half-morocco, £3 13*s.* 6*d.*

FLORIATED ORNAMENTS. 31 Plates in Gold and Colours, royal 4to, half-morocco, £1 16*s.*

GOTHIC ORNAMENTS. 90 Plates, by J. D. HARDING and others. Royal 4to, half-bound, £1 16*s.*

ORNAMENTAL TIMBER GABLES. 30 Plates. Royal 4to, cloth extra, 18*s.*

SPECIMENS OF GOTHIC ARCHITECTURE, from Ancient Edifices in England. 114 Outline Plates by LE KEUX and others. With descriptive Letterpress and Glossary by E. J. WILLSON. Two Vols., 4to, half-morocco, £1 16*s.*

TRUE PRINCIPLES OF POINTED OR CHRISTIAN ARCHITECTURE. With 87 Illustrations. Small 4to, cloth extra, 10*s.* 6*d.*

PUNIANA; or, Thoughts Wise and Other-Why's. A New Collection of Riddles, Conundrums, Jokes, Sells, &c. In Two Series, each containing 3000 of the best Riddles, 10,000 most outrageous Puns, and upwards of fifty beautifully-executed Drawings by the Editor, the Hon. HUGH ROWLEY. Price of each Volume, in small 4to, blue and gold, gilt edges, 6*s*. *Each Series Complete in itself.*

"A witty, droll, and most amusing work, profusely and elegantly illustrated."—*Standard.*

PURSUIVANT OF ARMS (The); or, Heraldry founded upon Facts. A Popular Guide to the Science of Heraldry. By J. R. PLANCHÉ, Esq., Somerset Herald. To which are added, Essays on the BADGES OF THE HOUSES OF LANCASTER AND YORK. With Coloured Frontispiece, five full-page Plates, and about 200 Illustrations. Crown 8vo, cloth extra, gilt, 7*s*. 6*d*.

QUEENS AND KINGS, AND OTHER THINGS: A Rare and Choice Collection of Pictures, Poetry, and strange but veritable Histories, designed and written by the Princess HESSE-SCHWARZBOURG. Imprinted in gold and many colours by the Brothers DALZIEL, at their Camden Press. Imperial 4to, cloth gilt and gilt edges, £1 1*s*.

RABELAIS' WORKS. Faithfully translated from the French, with variorum Notes, and numerous Characteristic Illustrations by GUSTAVE DORÉ. Crown 8vo, cloth extra, 700 pages, 7*s*. 6*d*.

READE'S (Winwood) THE OUTCAST. Cr. 8vo, cloth extra, 5*s*.

"He relaxed his mind in his leisure hours by the creation of a new religion."—*Standard.*

"A work of very considerable power, written with great pathos and evident earnestness."—*Athenæum.*

REMARKABLE TRIALS AND NOTORIOUS CHARACTERS. From "Half-Hanged Smith," 1700, to Oxford, who shot at the Queen, 1840. By Captain L. BENSON. With nearly Fifty spirited full-page Engravings by PHIZ. Crown 8vo, cloth extra, gilt, 7*s*. 6*d*.

ROLL OF BATTLE ABBEY; or, A List of the Principal Warriors who came over from Normandy with William the Conqueror, and Settled in this Country, A.D. 1066–7. Printed on fine plate paper, nearly three feet by two, with the principal Arms emblazoned in Gold and Colours. Price 5*s*.

ROLL OF CAERLAVEROCK, the Oldest Heraldic Roll; including the Original Anglo-Norman Poem, and an English Translation of the MS. in the British Museum. By THOMAS WRIGHT, M.A. The Arms emblazoned in Gold and Colours. In 4to, very handsomely printed, extra gold cloth, 12*s*.

ROMAN CATHOLICS IN THE COUNTY OF YORK IN 1604 (A List of). Transcribed from the MS. in the Bodleian Library, and Edited, with Notes, by EDWARD PEACOCK, F.S.A. Small 4to, cloth extra, 15*s*.

ROSCOE'S LIFE AND PONTIFICATE OF LEO THE TENTH. Edited by his Son, THOMAS ROSCOE. Two Vols., 8vo, with Portraits and numerous Plates, cloth extra, 18*s*.

*** Also, an Edition in One Vol. 16mo, cloth extra, price 3*s*.

ROSCOE'S LIFE OF LORENZO DE' MEDICI, called "THE MAGNIFICENT." A New and much improved Edition. Edited by his Son, THOMAS ROSCOE. Demy 8vo, with Portraits and numerous Plates, cloth extra, 9*s*.

ROSS'S (C. H.) STORY OF A HONEYMOON. With numerous Illustrations by the Author. Fcap. 8vo, illustrated boards, 2*s*.

ROWLANDSON (Thomas): HIS LIFE AND TIMES. With the History of his Caricatures, and the Key to their Meaning. With very numerous full-page Plates and Wood Engravings. Demy 4to, cloth extra, gilt and gilt edges, 31*s.* 6*d.* [*In preparation.*

SAINT-SIMON (MEMOIRS OF THE DUKE OF), during the Reign of Louis the Fourteenth and the Regency. Translated from the French and Edited by BAYLE ST. JOHN. A New Edition, in Three Vols., 8vo, with numerous Steel-plate Illustrations. [*In preparation.*

SALA (George Augustus) ON COOKERY IN ITS HISTORICAL ASPECT. With very numerous Illustrations by the AUTHOR. Crown 4to, cloth extra, gilt. [*In preparation.*

SEVEN GENERATIONS OF EXECUTIONERS.

SANSON FAMILY. Memoirs of the, compiled from Private Documents in the possession of the Family (1688-1847), by HENRI SANSON. Translated from the French, with an Introduction by CAMILLE BARRÈRE. Two Vols., 8vo, cloth extra. [*In the press.*

*** *Sanson was the hereditary French executioner, who officiated at the decapitation of Louis XVI.*

SCHOLA ITALICA; or, Engravings of the finest Pictures in the Galleries at Rome. Imperial folio, with 40 beautiful Engravings after MICHAEL ANGELO, RAPHAEL, TITIAN, CARACCI, GUIDO, PARMIGIANO, &c., by VOLPATO and others, half-bound morocco extra, £2 12*s.* 6*d.*

SCHOPENHAUER'S THE WORLD AS WILL AND IMAGINATION. Translated by Dr. FRANZ HÜFFER, Author of "Richard Wagner and the Music of the Future." [*In preparation.*

SCOTT'S COMMENTARY ON THE HOLY BIBLE. With the Author's Last Corrections, and beautiful Illustrations and Maps. Three Vols., imperial 8vo, cloth extra, £1 16*s.*

"SECRET OUT" SERIES.

Crown 8vo, cloth extra, profusely Illustrated, price 4*s.* 6*d.* each.

ART OF AMUSING: A Collection of Graceful Arts, Games, Tricks, Puzzles, and Charades. By FRANK BELLEW. 300 Illustrations.

HANKY-PANKY: Very Easy Tricks, Very Difficult Tricks, White Magic, Sleight of Hand. Edited by W. H. CREMER. 200 Illustrations.

MAGICIAN'S OWN BOOK: Performances with Cups and Balls, Eggs, Hats, Handkerchiefs, &c. All from Actual Experience. Edited by W. H. CREMER. 200 Illustrations.

MAGIC NO MYSTERY: Tricks with Cards, Dice, Balls, &c., with fully descriptive Directions. Numerous Illustrations. [*In the press.*

MERRY CIRCLE (The): A Book of New Intellectual Games and Amusements. By CLARA BELLEW. Numerous Illustrations.

SECRET OUT: One Thousand Tricks with Cards, and other Recreations; with entertaining Experiments in Drawing-room or "White Magic." By W. H. CREMER. 300 Engravings.

SEYMOUR'S (Robert) HUMOROUS SKETCHES. 86 Clever and Amusing Caricature Etchings on Steel, with Letterpress Commentary by ALFRED CROWQUILL. A New Edition, with Biographical Notice, and Descriptive List of Plates. Royal 8vo, cloth extra, gilt edges, 15*s.*

SHAKESPEARE.—THE FIRST FOLIO. Mr. WILLIAM SHAKESPEARE'S Comedies, Histories, and Tragedies. Published according to the true Origina Copies. London, Printed by ISAAC IAGGARD and ED. BLOUNT. 1623.—An exact Reproduction of the extremely rare Original, in reduced facsimile by a photographic process—thus ensuring the strictest accuracy in every detail. Small 8vo, half Roxburghe, 10*s.* 6*d.* [*In the press.*

SHAKESPEARE.—THE LANSDOWNE EDITION. Beautifully printed in red and black, in small but very clear type. Post 8vo, with engraved facsimile of DROESHOUT'S Portrait, cloth extra, gilt, gilt edges, 14*s.*; or, illustrated by 37 beautiful Steel Plates, after STOTHARD, cloth extra, gilt, gilt edges, 18*s.*

SHAKESPEARE, THE SCHOOL OF. Including "The Life and Death of Captain Thomas Stukeley," with a New Life of Stucley, from Unpublished Sources; "A Warning for Fair Women," with a Reprint of the Account of the Murder; "Nobody and Somebody;" "The Cobbler's Prophecy;" "Histriomastix;" "The Prodigal Son," &c. Edited, with Introductions and Notes, by R. SIMPSON, Author of "An Introduction to the Philosophy of Shakespeare's Sonnets." Two Vols., crown 8vo, cloth extra. [*In the press.*

SHAW'S ILLUMINATED WORKS.

ALPHABETS, NUMERALS, AND DEVICES OF THE MIDDLE AGES. Selected from the finest existing Specimens. 4to, 48 Plates (26 Coloured), £2 2*s.*; Large Paper, imperial 4to, the Coloured Plates very highly finished and heightened with Gold, £4 4*s.* [*New Edition preparing.*

ANCIENT FURNITURE, drawn from existing Authorities. With Descriptions by Sir S. R. MEYRICK. 4to, 74 Plates, half-morocco, £1 11*s.* 6*d.*; or, with some Plates Coloured, 4to, half-morocco, £2 2*s.*; Large Paper copies, imperial 4to, all the Plates extra finished in opaque Colours, half-morocco extra, £4 14*s.* 6*d.*

DECORATIVE ARTS OF THE MIDDLE AGES. Exhibiting, in 41 Plates and numerous beautiful Woodcuts, choice Specimens of the various kinds of Ancient Enamel, Metal Work, Wood Carvings, Paintings on Stained Glass, Venetian Glass, Initial Illuminations, Embroidery, Fictile Ware, Bookbinding, &c.; with elegant Initial Letters to the various Descriptions. Imperial 8vo, half-morocco extra, £1 8*s.*

DRESSES AND DECORATIONS OF THE MIDDLE AGES, from the Seventh to the Seventeenth Centuries. 94 Plates, beautifully Coloured, a profusion of Initial Letters, and Examples of Curious Ornament, with Historical Introduction and Descriptive Text. Two Vols., imperial 8vo, half-Roxburghe, £5 5*s.*

ELIZABETHAN ARCHITECTURE (DETAILS OF). With Descriptive Letterpress by T. MOULE. 4to, 60 Plates, half-morocco, £1 5*s.*; Large Paper, imperial 4to, several of the Plates Coloured, half-morocco, £2 12*s.* 6*d.*

ENCYCLOPÆDIA OF ORNAMENT. Select Examples from the purest and best Specimens of all kinds and all Ages. 4to, 59 Plates, half-morocco, £1 1*s.*; Large Paper copies, imperial 4to, with all the Plates Coloured, half-morocco, £2 12*s.* 6*d.*

ILLUMINATED ORNAMENTS OF THE MIDDLE AGES, from the Sixth to the Seventeenth Century. Selected from Missals, MSS., and early printed Books. 66 Plates, carefully coloured from the Originals, with Descriptions by Sir F. MADDEN, Keeper of MSS., Brit. Mus. 4to, half-Roxburghe, £3 13*s.* 6*d.*; Large Paper copies, the Plates finished with opaque Colours and illuminated with Gold, imperial 4to, half-Roxburghe, £7 7*s.*

LUTON CHAPEL: A Series of 20 highly-finished Line Engravings of Gothic Architecture and Ornaments. Imperial folio, India Proofs, half-morocco, £2 8*s.*

ORNAMENTAL METAL WORK: A Series of 50 Copperplates, several Coloured. 4to, half-morocco, 18*s.*

SHAW AND BRIDGENS' DESIGNS FOR FURNITURE, with Candelabra and Interior Decoration. 60 Plates, royal 4to, half-morocco, £1 1*s.* Large Paper, imperial 4to, the Plates Coloured, half-morocco, £2 8*s.*

SHELLEY'S EARLY LIFE. From Original Sources. With Curious Incidents, Letters, and Writings, now First Collected. By D. F. MACCARTHY Crown 8vo, with Illustrations, cloth extra, 7*s.* 6*d.*

SHERIDAN'S COMPLETE WORKS, with Life and Anecdotes. Including his Dramatic Writings, printed from the Original Editions, his Works in Prose and Poetry, Translations, Speeches, Jokes, Puns, &c.; with a Collection of Sheridaniana. Crown 8vo, cloth extra, gilt, with 10 full-page Tinted Illustrations, 7*s.* 6*d.*

"Whatever Sheridan has done, has been, *par excellence*, always the *best* of its kind. He has written the best comedy (School for Scandal, the *best* drama (the Duenna), the *best* farce (the Critic), and the *best* address (Monologue on Garrick): and, to crown all, delivered the very best oration (the famous Begum Speech) ever conceived or heard in this country."—BYRON.

"The editor has brought together within a manageable compass not only the seven plays by which Sheridan is best known, but a collection also of his poetical pieces which are less familiar to the public, sketches of unfinished dramas, selections from his reported witticisms, and extracts from his principal speeches. To these is prefixed a short but well-written memoir, giving the chief facts in Sheridan's literary and political career: so that with this volume in his hand, the student may consider himself tolerably well furnished with all that is necessary for a general comprehension of the subject of it."—*Pall Mall Gazette.*

SIGNBOARDS: Their History. With Anecdotes of Famous Taverns and Remarkable Characters. By JACOB LARWOOD and JOHN CAMDEN HOTTEN. With nearly 100 Illustrations. SEVENTH EDITION. Crown 8vo, cloth extra, 7*s.* 6*d.*

"Even if we were ever so maliciously inclined, we could not pick out all Messrs. Larwood and Hotten's plums, because the good things are so numerous as to defy the most wholesale depredation."—*The Times.*

SILVESTRE'S UNIVERSAL PALÆOGRAPHY; or, A Collection of Facsimiles of the Writings of every Age. Containing upwards of 300 large and beautifully executed Facsimiles, taken from Missals and other MSS., richly Illuminated in the finest style of art. A New Edition, arranged under the direction of Sir F. MADDEN, Keeper of MSS., Brit. Mus. Two Vols., atlas folio, half-morocco, gilt, £31 10*s.*

Also, a Volume of HISTORICAL AND DESCRIPTIVE LETTERPRESS, by CHAMPOLLION FIGEAC and CHAMPOLLION, Jun. Translated, with Additions, by Sir F. MADDEN. Two Vols., royal 8vo, half-morocco, gilt, £2 8*s.*

"This great work contains upwards of three hundred large and beautifully executed facsimiles of the finest and most interesting MSS. of various ages and nations, illuminated in the highest style of art. The cost of getting up this splendid publication was not far from £20,000."—*Allibone's Dict.*

"The great work on Palæography generally—one of the most sumptuous works of its class ever published."—*Chambers's Encyclopædia.*

SLANG DICTIONARY (The): Etymological, Historical, and Anecdotal. An ENTIRELY NEW EDITION, revised throughout, and considerably Enlarged. Crown 8vo, cloth extra, gilt, 6*s.* 6*d.*

"We are glad to see the Slang Dictionary reprinted and enlarged. From a high scientific point of view this book is not to be despised. Of course it cannot fail to be amusing also. It contains the very vocabulary of unrestrained humour, and oddity, and grotesqueness. In a word, it provides valuable material both for the student of language and the student of human nature."—*Academy.*

"In every way a great improvement on the edition of 1864. Its uses as a dictionary of the very vulgar tongue do not require to be explained."—*Notes and Queries.*

"Compiled with most exacting care, and based on the best authorities."—*Standard.*

SMITH'S HISTORICAL AND LITERARY CURIOSITIES: Containing Facsimiles of utographs, Scenes of Remarkable Events, Interesting Localities, Old Houses, Portraits, Illuminated and Missal Ornaments, Antiquities, &c. 4to, with 100 Plates (some Illuminated), half-morocco extra, £2 5*s.*

SMITH (Thomas Assheton), REMINISCENCES of the LATE; or, The Pursuits of an English Country Gentleman. By Sir J. E. EARDLEY WILMOT, Bart. New Edition, with Portrait, and plain and coloured Illustrations. Crown 8vo, cloth extra, 7*s.* 6*d.*

SMOKER'S TEXT-BOOK. By J. HAMER, F.R.S.L. Exquisitely printed from "silver-faced" type, cloth, very neat, gilt edges, 2*s.* 6*d.*

SOUTH'S (Dr. Robert) SERMONS. With Biographical Memoir, Analytical Tables, General Index, &c. Two Vols., royal 8vo, cloth extra, 15*s.*

SOUTHEY'S COMMON-PLACE BOOK. Edited by his Son-in-Law, J. W. WARTER. Second Edition. Four Vols., medium 8vo, with Portrait, cloth extra, £1 10*s.*

SOWERBY'S MANUAL OF CONCHOLOGY: A Complete Introduction to the Science. Illustrated by upwards of 650 etched Figures of Shells and numerous Woodcuts. With copious Explanations, Tables, Glossary, &c. 8vo, cloth extra, gilt, 15*s.*; or, the Plates beautifully Coloured, £1 8*s.*

SPECTATOR (The), with the Original Dedications, Notes, and a General Index. Demy 8vo, with Portrait of ADDISON, cloth extra, 9*s.*

STEDMAN'S (Edmund Clarence) VICTORIAN POETS: Critical Essays. Crown 8vo, cloth extra, 9*s.* [*In the press.*

Abstract of Contents:—The Period—Walter Savage Landor—Thomas Hood—Matthew Arnold—Bryan Waller Procter—Elizabeth Barrett Browning—Alfred Tennyson—Tennyson and Theocritus—Miscellaneous Poets—Robert Browning. Latter-Day Poets: Robert Buchanan—Dante Gabriel Rossetti—William Morris—Algernon Charles Swinburne.

STOTHARD'S MONUMENTAL EFFIGIES OF GREAT BRITAIN, selected from our Cathedrals and Churches. With Historical Description and Introduction, by JOHN KEMPE, F.S.A. A NEW EDITION, with a large body of Additional Notes by JOHN HEWITT. Imperial 4to, containing 147 beautifully finished Etchings, all Tinted, and some Illuminated in Gold and Colours, half-morocco, £9 9*s.*; Large Paper, the whole Illuminated in body-colours, half-morocco, £15 15*s.* [*In the press.*

STOW'S SURVEY OF LONDON, written in the Year 1598. Edited by W. J. THOMS, F.S.A. A New Edition, with Copperplate Illustrations, large 8vo, half-Roxburghe, price 9*s.*

STRUTT'S DRESSES AND HABITS OF THE ENGLISH, from the Establishment of the Saxons in Britain to the Present Time. With an Historical Inquiry into every branch of Costume, Ancient and Modern. New Edition, with Explanatory Notes by J. R. PLANCHÉ, Somerset Herald. Two Vols., royal 4to, with 153 Engravings from the most Authentic Sources, beautifully Coloured, half-Roxburghe, £6 6*s.*; or the Plates splendidly Illuminated in Silver and Opaque Colours, in the Missal style, half-Roxburghe, £15 15*s.*

STRUTT'S REGAL AND ECCLESIASTICAL ANTIQUITIES OF ENGLAND: Authentic Representations of all the English Monarchs, from Edward the Confessor to Henry the Eighth; with many Great Personages eminent under their several Reigns. New Edition, with critical Notes by J. R. PLANCHÉ, Somerset Herald. Royal 4to, with 72 Engravings from Manuscripts, Monuments, &c., beautifully Coloured, half-Roxburghe, £3 3*s.*; or the Plates splendidly Illuminated in Gold and Colours, half-morocco, £10 10*s.*

STRUTT'S SPORTS AND PASTIMES OF THE PEOPLE OF ENGLAND; including the Rural and Domestic Recreations, May Games, Mummeries, Shows, Processions, Pageants, and Pompous Spectacles, from the Earliest Period to the Present Time. Illustrated by One Hundred and Forty Engravings, in which are represented most of the popular Diversions, selected from Ancient Manuscripts. Edited by WILLIAM HONE, Author of the "Every-day Book." Crown 8vo, cloth extra, gilt, price 7*s.* 6*d.* A few LARGE PAPER COPIES have been prepared, uniform with the "Dresses," with an extra set of Copperplate Illustrations, carefully Coloured by hand, from the Originals, price 63*s.* [*In the press.*

STUBBS' ANATOMY OF THE HORSE. 24 fine Copperplate Engravings on a very large scale. Imperial folio, cloth extra, £1 1*s.*

SUMMER CRUISING IN THE SOUTH SEAS. By CHARLES WARREN STODDARD. With Twenty-five Illustrations by WALLIS MACKAY. Crown 8vo, cloth, extra gilt, 7*s.* 6*d.*

SWIFT'S CHOICE WORKS, in Prose and Verse. With Memoir, Portrait, and numerous Illustrations. Cr. 8vo, cl. extra, gilt, 7*s.* 6*d.* [*In the press.*

SYNTAX'S (Dr.) THREE TOURS. in Search of the Picturesque, in Search of Consolation, and in Search of a Wife. With the whole of ROWLANDSON'S droll full-page Illustrations, in Colours, and Life of the Author by J. C. HOTTEN. Medium 8vo, cloth extra, gilt, 7*s.* 6*d.*

SWINBURNE'S WORKS.

QUEEN MOTHER AND ROSAMOND. Fcap. 8vo, 5*s.*

ATALANTA IN CALYDON. A New Edition. Crown 8vo, 6*s.*

CHASTELARD: A Tragedy. Fcap. 8vo, 7*s.*

POEMS AND BALLADS. Fcap. 8vo, 9*s.*

WILLIAM BLAKE: A Critical Essay. With Facsimile Paintings, Coloured by Hand, after Drawings by BLAKE and his Wife. Demy 8vo, 16*s.*

SONGS BEFORE SUNRISE. Crown 8vo, 10*s.* 6*d.*

BOTHWELL: A Tragedy. Two Vols., crown 8vo, 12*s.* 6*d.*

GEORGE CHAPMAN: An Essay. Crown 8vo, 7*s.*

SONGS OF TWO NATIONS: DIRÆ, A SONG OF ITALY, ODE ON THE FRENCH REPUBLIC. Crown 8vo, 6*s.*

ESSAYS AND STUDIES. Crown 8vo, 12*s.*

Also, fcap. 8vo, cloth extra, price 3*s.* 6*d.*

ROSSETTI'S (W. M.) CRITICISM UPON SWINBURNE'S POEMS AND BALLADS.

TAYLOR'S HISTORY OF PLAYING CARDS: Ancient and Modern Games, Conjuring, Fortune-Telling, and Card Sharping, Gambling and Calculation, Cartomancy, Old Gaming-Houses, Card Revels and Blind Hookey, Picquet and Vingt-et-un, Whist and Cribbage, Tricks, &c. With Sixty curious Illustrations. Crown 8vo, cloth extra, gilt, price 7*s.* 6*d.*

THACKERAYANA: Notes and Anecdotes. Illustrated by a profusion of Sketches by WILLIAM MAKEPEACE THACKERAY, depicting Humorous Incidents in his School-life, and Favourite Characters in the books of his every-day reading. Large post 8vo, with Hundreds of Wood Engravings and Five Coloured Plates, from Mr. Thackeray's Original Drawings, cloth, full gilt, gilt top, 12*s.* 6*d.*

THEODORE HOOK'S CHOICE HUMOROUS WORKS, with his Ludicrous Adventures, Bons-mots, Puns, and Hoaxes. With a new Life of the Author, Portraits, Facsimiles, and Illustrations. Cr. 8vo, cloth extra, gilt, 7*s.* 6*d.*

THESEUS: A GREEK FAIRY LEGEND. Illustrated, in a series of Designs in Gold and Sepia, by JOHN MOYR SMITH. With Descriptive Text. Oblong folio, price 7*s.* 6*d.*

THIERS' HISTORY OF THE FRENCH REVOLUTION. Roy. 8vo, cloth extra, 15*s.*

"The History of the French Revolution by Thiers is a celebrated and popular book in France—and I believe in Europe. It combines the compactness and unity of the book, the order and arrangement of the journal, the simplicity of the biography, the valuable and minute details of the autobiography, and the enthusiasm, the passion, and the indignation of the pamphlet. There are in many parts of this great book, whole chapters which read as if they had been written with the sword." —JULES JANIN, *in the Athenæum.*

THIERS' HISTORY OF THE CONSULATE AND EMPIRE OF FRANCE UNDER NAPOLEON. Royal 8vo, cloth extra, 15*s*.

THOMSON'S SEASONS, and CASTLE OF INDOLENCE. With a Biographical and Critical Introduction by ALLAN CUNNINGHAM, and over 50 fine Illustrations on Steel and Wood. Crown 8vo, cloth extra, gilt, 7*s*. 6*d*. [*In the press.*

THORNBURY'S (Walter) HISTORICAL AND LEGENDARY BALLADS AND SONGS. Illustrated by J. WHISTLER, JOHN TENNIEL, A. F. SANDYS, W. SMALL, M. J. LAWLESS, J. D. WATSON, G. J. PINWELL, F. WALKER, T. R. MACQUOID, and others. Handsomely printed, crown 4to, cloth extra, gilt and gilt edges, 21*s*. [*In preparation.*

TIMBS' ENGLISH ECCENTRICS and ECCENTRICITIES: Stories of Wealth and Fashion, Delusions, Impostures and Fanatic Missions, Strange Sights and Sporting Scenes, Eccentric Artists, Theatrical Folks, Men of Letters, &c. By JOHN TIMBS, F.S.A. With nearly 50 Illustrations. Crown 8vo, cloth extra, 7*s*. 6*d*.

"The reader who would fain enjoy a harmless laugh in some very odd company might do much worse than take an occasional dip into 'English Eccentrics.' Beaux, preachers, authors, actors, monstrosities of the public shows, and leaders of religious impostures, will meet him here in infinite, almost perplexing, variety. The queer illustrations, from portraits and caricatures of the time, are admirably suited to the letterpress."—*Graphic.*

TIMBS' CLUBS AND CLUB LIFE IN LONDON. With ANECDOTES of its FAMOUS COFFEE HOUSES, HOSTELRIES, and TAVERNS. By JOHN TIMBS, F.S.A. With numerous Illustrations. Cr. 8vo, cloth extra, 7*s*. 6*d*.

TOURNEUR'S (Cyril) COLLECTED WORKS, including a unique Poem, entitled "The Transformed Metamorphosis;" and "Laugh and Lie Down; or, The World's Folly." Edited, with a Critical Preface, Introductions, and Notes, by J. CHURTON COLLINS. Post 8vo, cloth extra, 10*s*. 6*d*. [*In preparation.*

TURNER'S (J. M. W.) LIBER FLUVIORUM; or, River Scenery of France. 62 highly-finished Line Engravings by WILLMORE, GOODALL, MILLER, COUSENS, and other distinguished Artists. With descriptive Letterpress by LEITCH RITCHIE, and Memoir by ALARIC A. WATTS. Imperial 8vo, cloth extra, gilt edges, £1 11*s*. 6*d*.

TURNER (J. M. W.) and GIRTIN'S RIVER SCENERY. 20 beautiful Mezzotinto Plates, engraved on Steel by REYNOLDS, BROMLEY, LUPTON, and CHARLES TURNER, principally after the Drawings of J. M. W. TURNER. Small folio, in Portfolio, £1 11*s*. 6*d*.

TURNER'S (J. M. W.) LIFE AND CORRESPONDENCE. Founded upon Letters and Papers furnished by his Friends and Fellow-Academicians. By WALTER THORNBURY. New Edition, entirely rewritten and added to. With numerous Illustrations. Two Vols., 8vo, cloth extra. [*In preparation.*

TURNER GALLERY (The): A Series of Sixty Engravings from the Principal Works of JOSEPH MALLORD WILLIAM TURNER. With a Memoir and Illustrative Text by RALPH NICHOLSON WORNUM, Keeper and Secretary, National Gallery. Handsomely half-bound, India Proofs, royal folio, £10; Large Paper copies, Artists' India Proofs, elephant folio, £20.—A Descriptive Pamphlet will be sent upon application.

VAGABONDIANA; or, Anecdotes of Mendicant Wanderers through the Streets of London; with Portraits of the most Remarkable, drawn from the Life by JOHN THOMAS SMITH, late Keeper of the Prints in the British Museum. With Introduction by FRANCIS DOUCE, and Descriptive Text. With the Woodcuts and the 32 Plates, from the original Coppers. Crown 4to, half-Roxburghe, 12*s*. 6*d*.

VYNER'S NOTITIA VENATICA: A Treatise on Fox-Hunting, the General Management of Hounds, and the Diseases of Dogs; Distemper and Rabies; Kennel Lameness, &c. By ROBERT C. VYNER. Sixth Edition, Enlarged. With spirited Coloured Illustrations by ALKEN. Royal 8vo, cloth extra, 21*s.*

WALPOLE'S (Horace) ANECDOTES OF PAINTING IN ENGLAND. With some Account of the principal English Artists, and incidental Notices of Sculptors, Carvers, Enamellers, Architects, Medallists, Engravers, &c. With Additions by the Rev. JAMES DALLAWAY. New Edition, Revised and Edited, with Additional Notes, by RALPH N. WORNUM, Keeper and Secretary, National Gallery. Three Vols., 8vo, with upwards of 150 Portraits and Plates, cloth extra, £1 7*s.*

WALPOLE'S (Horace) ENTIRE CORRESPONDENCE. Chronologically arranged, with the Prefaces and Notes of CROKER, Lord DOVER, and others; the Notes of all previous Editors, and Additional Notes by PETER CUNNINGHAM. Nine Vols., 8vo, with numerous fine Portraits engraved on Steel, cloth extra, £4 1*s.*

"The charm which lurks in Horace Walpole's Letters is one for which we have no term; and our Gallic neighbours seem to have engrossed both the word and the quality—'elles sont piquantes,' to the highest degree. If you read but a sentence, you feel yourself spell-bound till you have read the volume."—*Quarterly Review.*

WALPOLE'S (Horace) ROYAL AND NOBLE AUTHORS OF ENGLAND, SCOTLAND, AND IRELAND; with Lists of their Works. A New Edition, Annotated, considerably Enlarged, and brought down to the Present Time. Illustrated by nearly 200 Copperplate Portraits. Six Vols., 8vo, cloth extra. [*In preparation.*

WALTON AND COTTON, ILLUSTRATED.—THE COMPLETE ANGLER; or, The Contemplative Man's Recreation: Being a Discourse of Rivers, Fish-ponds, Fish and Fishing, written by IZAAK WALTON; and Instructions how to Angle for a Trout or Grayling in a clear Stream, by CHARLES COTTON. With Original Memoirs and Notes by Sir HARRIS NICOLAS, K.C.M.G. With the 61 Plate Illustrations, precisely as in Pickering's two-volume Edition. Complete in One Volume, large crown 8vo, cloth antique, 7*s.* 6*d.*

WARRANT TO EXECUTE CHARLES I. An exact Facsimile of this important Document, with the Fifty-nine Signatures of the Regicides, and corresponding Seals, on paper to imitate the Original, 22 in. by 14 in. Price 2*s.*

WARRANT TO EXECUTE MARY QUEEN OF SCOTS. An exact Facsimile of this important Document, including the Signature of Queen Elizabeth and Facsimile of the Great Seal, on tinted paper, to imitate the Original MS. Price 2*s.*

WATERFORD ROLL (The).—Illuminated Charter-Roll of Waterford, Temp. Richard II. The Illuminations accurately Traced and Coloured for the Work from a Copy carefully made by the late GEORGE V. DU NOYER, Esq., M.R.I.A. Those Charters which have not already appeared in print will be edited by the Rev. JAMES GRAVES, A.B., M.R.I.A. Imperial 4to, cloth extra, gilt, 36*s.* [*Nearly ready.*

WELLS' JOSEPH AND HIS BRETHREN: A Dramatic Poem. By CHARLES O. WELLS. With an Introductory Essay by ALGERNON CHARLES SWINBURNE. Crown 8vo, cloth extra, 8*s.* [*In the press.*

WESTWOOD'S PALÆOGRAPHIA SACRA PICTORIA: being a Series of Illustrations of the Ancient Versions of the Bible, copied from Illuminated Manuscripts, executed between the Fourth and Sixteenth Centuries. Royal 4to, with 50 beautifully Illuminated Plates, half-bound morocco, £3 10*s.*

WILD'S ENGLISH CATHEDRALS. Twelve select examples of the Ecclesiastical Architecture of the Middle Ages; beautifully coloured, after the Original Drawings by CHARLES WILD. Imperial folio, in portfolio, £4 4*s.*

WILD'S FOREIGN CATHEDRALS. Twelve fine Plates, imperial folio, coloured, after the Original Drawings, by CHARLES WILD. In portfolio, £4 4*s.*

"These splendid plates are unequalled, whether bound as a volume, treasured in a portfolio, or framed for universal admiration."—*Athenæum.*

WILSON'S AMERICAN ORNITHOLOGY; or, Natural History of the Birds of the United States; with the Continuation by Prince CHARLES LUCIAN BONAPARTE. NEW AND ENLARGED EDITION, completed by the insertion of above One Hundred Birds omitted in the original Work, and Illustrated by valuable Notes, and Life of the Author, by Sir WILLIAM JARDINE. Three Vols., 8vo, with a fine Portrait of WILSON, and 103 Plates, exhibiting nearly four hundred figures of Birds accurately engraved and beautifully printed in Colours, half-bound morocco. A few Large Paper copies will also be issued, with the Plates all carefully Coloured by hand. [*In the press.*

"The History of American Birds by Alexander Wilson is equal in elegance to the most distinguished of our own splendid works on Ornithology."—CUVIER.

WILSON'S FRENCH-ENGLISH AND ENGLISH-FRENCH DICTIONARY; containing full Explanations, Definitions, Synonyms, Idioms, Proverbs, Terms of Art and Science, and Rules for the Pronunciation of each Language. Compiled from the Dictionaries of the French Academy, BOYER, CHAMBAUD, GARNIER, LAVEAUX, DES CARRIÈRES and FAIN, JOHNSON, and WALKER. Imperial 8vo, 1,323 closely-printed pages, cloth extra, 15*s.*

WONDERFUL CHARACTERS: Memoirs and Anecdotes of Remarkable and Eccentric Persons of every Age and Nation. By HENRY WILSON and JAMES CAULFIELD. Crown 8vo, cloth extra, with 61 full-page Engravings, 7*s.* 6*d.*

WRIGHT'S (Andrew) COURT-HAND RESTORED; or, Student's Assistant in Reading Old Deeds, Charters, Records, &c. Folio, half-morocco, 10*s.* 6*d.*

WRIGHT'S CARICATURE HISTORY of the GEORGES (House of Hanover). With 400 Pictures, Caricatures, Squibs, Broadsides, Window Pictures, &c. By THOMAS WRIGHT, Esq., M.A., F.S.A. Crown 8vo, cloth extra, 7*s.* 6*d.*

"Emphatically one of the liveliest of books, as also one of the most interesting. Has the twofold merit of being at once amusing and edifying."—*Morning Post.*

WRIGHT'S HISTORY OF CARICATURE AND OF THE GROTESQUE IN ART, LITERATURE, SCULPTURE, AND PAINTING, from the Earliest Times to the Present Day. By THOMAS WRIGHT, M.A., F.S.A. Profusely Illustrated by F. W. FAIRHOLT, F.S.A. Large post 8vo, cloth extra, gilt, 7*s.* 6*d.*

"Almost overwhelms us with its infinite research. Mr. Wright dexterously guides the reader to a full survey of our English caricature, from its earliest efforts to the full-blown blossoms of a Rowlandson or a Gillray. The excellent illustrations of Mr. Fairholt add greatly to the value of the volume."—*Graphic.*

"A very amusing and instructive volume."—*Saturday Review.*

XENOPHON'S COMPLETE WORKS. Translated into English. Demy 8vo, with Steel-plate Portrait, a thick volume of 770 pages, 12*s.*

YANKEE DROLLERIES. Edited, with Introduction, by GEORGE AUGUSTUS SALA. In Three Parts, each Complete in itself. Crown 8vo, cloth extra, 3*s.* 6*d.* per Vol.

J. OGDEN AND CO., PRINTERS, 172, ST. JOHN STREET, E.C.

www.ingramcontent.com/pod-product-compliance
Lightning Source LLC
Chambersburg PA
CBHW031346070726
47496CB00017B/1806

9783337032203